. . . Willow could think, the older woman reached . . . laptop, and disconnected the modem line. She tucked the computer under her arm. "I see what you're doing," Sheila Rosenberg said. "You're challenging me. But I will *not* have you communicating with your . . . cyber-coven or what have you."

Willow brought her legs around and sat upright. "Coven? What happened to me being delusional and acting out?"

"Well, that was before I talked in depth with Ms. Summers and her associates. It seems I've been rather close-minded." She waved a hand in the air.

Willow brightened. "So you believe me?"

Her mother's face softened, and she smiled sweetly. "I believe you, dear." She hesitated for the briefest of moments. "Now all I can do is let you go with love."

Willow's mouth dropped open. "Let me go? What does that mean? Mom?"

Her mother didn't answer. Instead she turned and walked out of Willow's room, shut the door behind herself—

—and locked it.

Buffy the Vampire Slayer™

Available from ARCHWAY Paperbacks and POCKET PULSE

Buffy the Vampire Slayer adult books

Available from POCKET BOOKS

BUFFY
THE VAMPIRE
SLAYER™

THE WILLOW FILES
Vol. 2

A novelization by Yvonne Navarro
Based on the hit TV series created by Joss Whedon
Based on the teleplays "Gingerbread" by Jane Espenson
(story by Thania St. John and Jane Espenson),
"Doppelgängland" by Joss Whedon,
and "Choices" by David Fury

POCKET PULSE
New York London Toronto Sydney Singapore

This book is a work of fiction. Names, characters, places and incidents are products of the author's imagination or are used fictitiously. Any resemblance to actual events or locales or persons, living or dead, is entirely coincidental.

An *Original* Publication of POCKET BOOKS

 POCKET PULSE, published by
Pocket Books, a division of Simon & Schuster, Inc.
1230 Avenue of the Americas, New York, NY 10020

™ and © 2001 Twentieth Century Fox Film Corporation. All rights reserved.

ISBN: 0-7434-0043-7

First Pocket Pulse printing February 2001

10 9 8 7 6 5 4 3 2 1

POCKET PULSE and colophon are registered trademarks of Simon & Schuster, Inc.

Printed in the U.S.A.

This one's for
Robyn Fielder,
my second sister and savior.

Acknowledgments

Thanks to Christopher Golden, Micol Ostow, Lisa Clancy, Sephera Giron, Robyn Fielder, Don VanderSluis, and, as always, my dad, Marty Cochran, for providing the Land of Dad's Free Rent, Food, and Phone.

THE FILES

DAILY JOURNAL ENTRY:

Okay, so I haven't been as good at keeping my computer journal up to date as I thought I'd be.

It's not like we haven't been busy around here, you know. In fact, things have been like ultra, super-mondo busy, with stuff happening at twice the usual Sunnydale weird-rate. Think I'm joking? We have *two* Slayers now—the new one is called Faith, and she just kind of . . . showed up one evening in the Bronze and started vamp pummeling that same night. She's sort of wild and, well, she doesn't follow orders very well—Giles seems pretty freaked a lot of the time, since his constant grown-up attempt at the authority thing is pretty much lost on Faith. As for Buffy . . . she's different now. I know that the time she spent away from Sunnydale last summer had a big impact on her mind and heart, but Faith has affected her in a different way. It's hard to put my finger on it, but she seems half dismayed by the way Faith acts, but half competitive, too . . . like she has to constantly prove she's still worth something now.

Even with two Slayers, it doesn't seem like anyone's managed to sneak totally past the Hellmouth's influence. Not long after Faith got here, this guy named Scott who was sweet on Buffy for a while lost a couple of good friends, Pete and Debbie, to the special brand of evil influence that seeps all through this town. Pete was so obsessed with being perfect for Debbie that he just couldn't see beyond the illusion he had about what was right and what was wrong, and in the end it killed them both. The whole Scott-as-a-potential-Buffy-boyfriend thing blew up big-time when Angel came back from Hell at the same time I nearly lost Oz.

No, the vampires didn't almost get him, and that creepy werewolf hunter Gib Cain didn't come skulking back into town. I've thought a lot of things about myself—like sometimes I'm so dependable and predictable that I even turn *invisible*—but I always thought I was at least smart and in control. I guess sometimes even the smartest of us, well, lose it, just mess up the best of what we've got going without really understanding why we're doing what we're doing at the time, a whacked-out version of that urge to push that big red button labeled "Don't Push Me!" You know which one—it's usually tied to the bomb that blows up everything worthwhile in your existence.

See, this thing I had for Xander all

these years . . . and, it turns out, he always had this kind of thing for me, too, you know? But he never said or did anything, and neither did I. But then we were trying to get ready for homecoming, and we just—

Okay, we ended up, somehow, kissing. To make it even worse, after that, it seemed like we couldn't *not* grab a smoochie or two every chance we got, or play footsie in class, or whatever. I'm not even sure how or why, but there it was, this . . . *thing* between us, except it wasn't really a *thing*, just a freaky sort of delayed attraction. I tried concocting a spell to cool things off, but I never did pull it together in time, and my Wiccan skills are still growing—they need a little, like, fine-tuning or whatever. Not long after was when Cordelia and Oz found out about Xander and me . . . except they did it the hard way.

As in a direct eye-view when Xander and I thought we were alone.

It was pretty awful—Cordelia totally wigged and started to stalk off, but she was on these rickety stairs, and they, like, *collapsed*. She fell and got impaled by a piece of metal sticking out of the floor below us, and for one terrible moment we all thought she was dead. It turned out that she was okay, thank God, but poor Xander—

even while she was in the hospital, she wouldn't have anything to do with him, and now that she's out . . . she certainly won't forgive him. I'm really lucky, though; it took some time, but Oz decided to give us—me and him—another chance.

I'm just so sorry to see Xander suffer like this, especially since a lot of it is my fault—sharing the blame is the only honest thing. As for Cordelia . . . she can be so venomous to begin with, but I can't help but think it might have gone a little better for her if she'd had her old friends to give her support . . . well, whatever kind of support you get from people like that, anyway. But they pretty much abandoned her after Xander, and I guess they really reveled in their turn to lord it over Cordy—I heard there was a lot of verbal cutting directed at her.

A lot of people—okay, adults—claim that what goes around comes around. It might sound like a bunch of hooey, but so does a lot of stuff—like zombies, vampires, demons, and a whole host of other creepies that make the adults roll their eyes. So what if that saying is true? Because . . . well, divine payback scares me to death after what I did to Oz, even though he forgives me. How sad that we don't always see the wonderful in what we have when it's right in front of us, or worse, sometimes we let someone else cloud our view of what's out there....

/PRESS ENTER TO SAVE FILE/

FILE:
GINGERBREAD

PROLOGUE

In any other town, this could have—*would* have—been a pleasant stroll through a moonlit park. There was a nice, cool breeze gently ruffling the leaves overhead, the smell of freshly cut grass still lingered from an earlier Park District mowing, the street lamps cast a nice, inviting glow over everything, and the bugs were singing . . . or whatever it was that bugs did on a cool, early-spring evening.

But, of course, this was Sunnydale.

Blech, Buffy Summers thought as she eyed a heavy, close-cut bush a few feet off the walkway. It was trimmed in a decorative circular design, and its leaf-laden branches swung sideways for the second time, an unnatural movement and sound so different from the way the wind would have shaken them that it might as well have been a gong in Buffy's ears. Bloodsucker? Or demon? Buffy pulled out a stake and stepped toward it cautiously, but she stopped a few feet away. Until she knew exactly what she was dealing with, it was safer and more efficient to let it come to her—

"Is it a vampire?"

Buffy jumped and gripped her stake as her mother strode up from the other direction and stopped in front of her. Smiling, Joyce Summers held a brown paper bag and a thermos.

Buffy's mouth dropped open. "Mom? What are you doing here?"

Joyce hefted the lunch bag invitingly. "I brought you a snack. I thought it was about time I came out to watch, you know, the Slaying."

She wanted to *watch?* "Mom, you know the Slaying . . . it's kind of an alone thing." Her gaze cut past her mother and focused once more on the bush, the branches that were jerking around again. She slipped past Joyce and circled it, then realized her mom was trailing after her.

"But it's such a big part of your life," Joyce pointed out. "And I'd like to understand it. It's something we could share."

Buffy blinked. Slaying as a family activity—why did she think this was on a fast track to failure? "It's really pretty dull. Bam, boom, stick, poof. Not much to—"

The bloodsucker that leaped at her from behind the bush was suit-and-tie clad, nice and toothy. Buffy shoved her mother backward as she stepped up to meet the thing's attack. Blocking the vamp's downward punch, she spun and landed a solid roundhouse kick.

"Good, honey! Kill it!" Joyce shouted encouragingly.

The vampire stumbled backward, and Buffy jumped at it. Not quick enough—the thing got one of its feet up and caught her smack in the stomach. She went over its head like a rotating bicycle wheel and came down on her back behind it.

Her mother's excited voice propelled her back to her feet. "Buffy—he's over here!"

She wanted to give her mother a "look"—something along the order of "Bad Mom!" would've been doable—but there really wasn't time. She scrambled back to a fighting stance, but—

"Oh, my *God*—it's Mr. Sanderson from the bank!"

—her mother's incredulous words wiggled into her head and cut her concentration, making her efforts clumsy and uncoordinated. It required a double effort on her part, plus she had to take a few hard knocks, but she finally got the bloodsucker down with a leg sweep. In position at last, she raised her stake—

"Are you sure you have to kill him?" Joyce asked. "He opened my IRA."

Thrown off track, Buffy glanced at her mother in exasperation. "He's *not* Mr. Sanderson anymore, Mom. He's—"

The thing she'd been holding down bucked and was up in an instant.

"—getting away," Joyce finished for her.

This time, Buffy *did* get a "look" off to Joyce, a hard one. "Stay," she commanded harshly, then sprinted after the newly changed bank officer. Sanderson was fresh and awkward, completely inexperienced, and already she was closing on him—she had no doubt that in less than two minutes he'd be dust. Still, her mother was back there, alone and unprotected, so she had to get this over with as quickly as possible.

There was no telling what kind of mischief an unsupervised mom could get involved in around here.

* * *

Joyce watched her daughter chase after the vampire, feeling another pang of regret for the late Mr. Sanderson, intensified when she realized she'd never even known his first name. After a moment she glanced around and decided she didn't like this small clearing in the park—it was surrounded by too many hedges and trees, too quiet and isolated. Better, she thought as she shrugged a little against the chill, to move on ahead and into the playground area. It was more open and far less likely to offer hiding places to unsavory creatures of the night, plus just being surrounded by the children's play equipment made her feel better.

As if to reaffirm that, Joyce spied a toy truck a few feet in front of her. Small and battered, it was on its side in one of a dozen mini-puddles left by yesterday's rain, just inside the swing-set area. Somewhere behind her, she heard her daughter's yell, recognized it instantly as victorious—good for Buffy, she'd vanquished that nasty vampire. Satisfied, Joyce put the lunch bag and thermos on a bench and went over to the tiny truck, lifting the neglected toy from the water with a small smile as she straightened again. Perhaps someone would come back tomor—

She froze.

Forgotten, the toy truck slipped from her fingers and fell to the dirt as her shocked gaze focused on what was on the merry-go-round twenty feet away, then went to the figure on the gritty ground next to it.

"Oh . . . God," she whimpered. Against her will, against all reason, her feet carried her closer to the dreadful thing in front of her.

One child, a boy, lay on his side on the merry-go-round, his face serene and nearly as pale as his golden blond hair. The other was a girl, smaller and sprawled on the ground a few feet away, shining blond curls framing the cold, forever-silenced features of her face above a cute striped shirt.

The night surrounded Joyce suddenly, bringing not comfort but a deep, soul-chilling sadness at the sight of these two tiny dead children, each with a hand outflung as if in supplication, palm up, and painted with a dark and enigmatic symbol . . .

CHAPTER 1

On patrol, Weatherly Park was usually dark and quiet, the perfect place for a beastie in munch mode to lurk, a grand area to patrol and send that same beastie on a quick ride back to Hell. Now, however, it might as well have been high noon—the place was filled with portable lights, noise, and people, and all of them were running on this bizarre sort of contained energy that was half panic, half shocked numbness. Police officers moved from squad car to squad car and then to the waiting coroner's van, talking into static-filled radios and stringing crime tape while a police photographer recorded the terrible deed from all angles.

Buffy couldn't believe it. She was accustomed to seeing vamps, even vamp children; while she'd never gotten used to it, she *had* reached a point where she could deal—she knew the cause and the culprit that brought about the birth of a baby bloodsucker, and she knew, too, that she was not only releasing the child's physical form from demonic entrapment but saving others at the same time.

But this . . .

The boy was maybe eight years old, the girl possibly six. Brother and sister, without a doubt—had there not been that obvious age difference, they looked so much alike they might have been Teutonic twins. The shining blond hair hinted at a Scandinavian or German heritage, but the police would verify that later, when the parents were given the terrible news that their children would never return. She hoped they'd be able to forget the sight of the small bodies with the deathly pale skin and blue-tinged lips, that they'd be able to remember how they'd been in life rather than in death.

The officer she'd been talking to made a final notation on his clipboard, then nodded at her and angled away. Buffy hugged herself for a moment, then made her way to her mother's side. Joyce didn't even move when Buffy walked up, just stood there, staring into space. "They said we can go home now," Buffy said softly.

For a moment Joyce said nothing, then her eyes met Buffy's. "They were little kids," she said in a small voice. "Did you see them? So . . . tiny."

"I saw."

Joyce's expression was devastated. "Who would do something like this? I never—" She choked a little and hung her head, fighting back tears.

"I'm so sorry you had to see this," Buffy said. She touched her mother's arm. "But it's going to be okay."

Joyce only looked at her. "How?"

"I'll find whatever did this," Buffy said without hesitation.

Still, it was obvious her mother wasn't comforted. "I

guess. It's just that you can't . . ." She paused, then drew in a breath. "You can't make it *right*." Her shoulders began to shake.

Buffy put her arms out and pulled her mother into a tight hug. "It's okay," she said as soothingly as she could. "I'll take care of everything. I promise, Mom. Just try to calm down."

"Don't tell me to calm down!"

On the library stairs above her, Rupert Giles recoiled and stepped back. "I only meant—"

"They were *kids,* Giles." Buffy was so angry she felt her fists clench. "Little kids. You don't know what it was like to *see* them there. My mom—she can't even *talk.*"

Her Watcher stood there, waiting. "I'm sorry, Buffy. I just want to help."

She took a breath to continue her tirade, then realized how useless that was. Her shoulders slumped a bit. "I know."

Giles came the rest of the way down the stairs, and she followed him over to the library table. "Do we know anything about how? It wasn't the vampire—"

Buffy shook her head, stopping the rest of his question. "There were no marks." She started to say something else as Giles lifted his cup of tea, then her eyes widened. "Wait—I mean, there *was* a mark. A symbol." There was an old-looking piece of paper in front of her, and she snatched a marker from the counter and reached for it.

"Ooh—" For balancing a cup of tea in one hand, Giles moved pretty quickly as he slid the paper out of range before the tip of her drawing pen could touch down. "Uh . . . twelfth-century papal encyclical," he explained as he offered her a notepad instead. "Try this."

Buffy barely registered his words, so intent was she on remembering what she'd seen and getting it down properly. "It was on their hands," she told him as she worked. "The cops are keeping it quiet, but I got a good look at it." After a few moments, she shoved the notepad back to the librarian and pointed at the symbol she'd drawn, a triangle cut through its upper half by a horizontal line with a downward curve at each end.

"Find the thing that uses this symbol, and point me at it."

Giles studied it. "Hmmmm."

Buffy frowned at him when he didn't continue. "Hmmm what? Giles, *speak.*"

"What? Oh, sorry." Her Watcher tilted his head as he considered her drawing. "It's just . . . I wonder if we're looking for a *thing* at all. The use of a symbol on a victim like this suggests a ritual murder, an occult sacrifice by a group."

Buffy's eyes darkened. "A group of . . . human beings? Someone with a *soul* did this?"

"I'm afraid so," Giles told her as he stood and went over to one of the bookcases to scan the titles.

She sat there for a second, not even able to form words as this concept made her feel colder inside than she had in a long time. "Okay," she said at last, then sucked in a lungful of air. "So while you're looking for the meaning of the symbol thingy, maybe you could turn up a loophole in that 'Slayers don't kill people' rule."

Squatting by the bookcase, Giles swiveled and looked at her in alarm before standing and returning to her side. "Buffy, this is a dreadful crime, I know," he said gently. "You have every right to be upset. However, I wonder if you're not letting yourself get a shade more personal because of your mother's involvement."

"Oh, it's *completely* personal. Giles, find me the people who did this. *Please.*"

Without another word, Buffy turned and strode out of the library, feeling Giles's gaze on her back before he went back to his beloved research books.

Willow Rosenberg stood in the crowded cafeteria with her friend Amy and scanned the tables, looking for an empty one. A few feet away she could hear Xander Harris trying, somewhat desperately, to make conversation with her boyfriend, Oz.

"So," Xander said with strategic brightness. "A burrito."

Oz glanced at him as he dropped the school's version of genuine Mexican grub onto his tray. His expression never changed. "This is a burrito," he agreed.

"Damn straight," Xander said.

Awkward, Willow thought as she watched them head for the cashier. Sooner or later the stiffness fueled by the guilt she and Xander felt would wear off and everyone would get back to normal . . . wouldn't they? Then again, maybe not—Cordelia had turned into the Ice Queen toward Xander and the rest of the Slayerettes as well. For her, there were some things you just didn't go back to, and obviously Xander was in that group.

Off to the side, she glimpsed Xander and Oz snag a table, so she and Amy angled that way. "Hi, Oz," she said, and smiled. She glanced at Xander and nodded. "Xander."

There were hi's and heys all the way around, then Xander peered at Amy. "Hey, Amy—like the new hair." She had recently darkened her normally blond bob to brunet.

Amy smiled as Oz looked to Willow. "I haven't seen you all day. Where've you been?"

She opened her mouth to answer, but Xander cut her off. "Not with me!" he announced. "No, sir. Ask anyone." They all stared at him, and he floundered around a final denial. "Noooo."

More silence, and Willow wished she could think of something cheerful and witty to say, anything to start the conversation over again. Then, thank goodness, Oz sat forward and saved the day.

"So," her boyfriend said. "Buffy's birthday is next week."

Xander's sigh of relief was audible. "Oh—yeah. Good." He grinned slyly. "I've been pondering gift options—"

Willow's eyes widened as she glimpsed something behind Xander. "Shhhhh!"

"Oh, come on," Xander griped. "We just got a topic here."

"Hi, *Buffy*," Willow said purposefully. She smiled widely at her friend.

"Buffy!" Xander said. Surprised, he still recovered admirably, scooting out of his chair and offering it to her. "So, what's up?" He pulled an empty seat over from another table.

Buffy sat, her face somber. "You guys didn't hear?"

Xander frowned slightly. "Hear what?"

"About the murders," Buffy said quietly. There were shadows beneath her eyes, and Willow noticed she was lunch-free. "Somebody killed two little kids."

Willow gasped. "Oh, no!"

Her best friend pressed her lips together. "They were,

like, seven or eight years old. My mom found the bodies during patrol last night."

"Oh, my God," Amy said.

"Kids?" Oz asked. Even he looked stunned.

Xander was puzzled. "How is it your mom was there?"

Buffy shook her head in disbelief. "More bad—she picked last night, of all nights, for a surprise 'bonding' visit."

Willow tried to process this. "God . . . your mom would actually take the time to do that with you?" When all her friends eyed her instead of answering, she realized her blunder. "Which . . . really isn't the point of the story, is it?" She pinkened.

Buffy sighed. "No. The point is she's *completely* wigging."

"Who's wigging?"

When they realized Joyce Summers was standing behind Buffy, their jerks of surprise were so perfectly timed they could have been choreographed. "Uh, everyone," Buffy managed. She stood, clearly nervous. "You know, because of . . . what happened."

Mrs. Summers nodded listlessly. "Oh, it's *so* awful. I had bad dreams about it all night."

The haunted expression on the older woman's face made Willow exchange glances with her friends. "Hi, Mrs. Summers," Willow said, hoping to derail her train of thought. Xander and Oz put in their mumbled one-word greetings while Amy echoed Willow.

"Hello, everybody," Joyce said, but her heart obviously wasn't in it. She turned to her daughter. "Buffy, have you talked with Mr. Giles yet about who could have done it?"

Buffy looked uncomfortable. "Uh, yeah. He thinks it might be something ritual . . . occult. He's still looking.

In the meantime, we're going to add to my patrols. You know, keep an eye out—"

"Occult?" Joyce was clearly appalled. "Like witches?"

Amy's mouth fell open, and she twitched at the same time as Willow's milk suddenly backed up in her throat and made her choke and start coughing. After a second or two, she pulled it together. "Sorry," she got out. "Phlegm—too much dairy."

Joyce's gaze stopped on her briefly. "Oh, I know you kids think that stuff is cool. Buffy told me you dabble—"

"Absolutely," Willow agreed, trying to sound happy-go-lucky. "That's me. I'm a dabbler."

"But anybody who could do this isn't cool," Joyce continued. Her breathing was getting shorter and faster with every word. "Anybody who could do *this* has to be a *monster*. It—"

"You know what?" Buffy interrupted. She put a hand on her mom's arm as she glanced back at her friends. "Could you guys excuse us for a little bit?"

Willow and the others nodded as Buffy pulled her mom toward the cafeteria exit. Mrs. Summers blinked, then gave them all a little wave. "Nice to see you, kids," she said absently, then let Buffy steer her away.

"What a burn," Xander commented as they watched the two leave. "Buff's mom was just starting to accept the Slayer thing. Now she's going to be double-freaked."

Willow exchanged a meaningful glance with Amy. "Makes me glad my mother doesn't know about my extracurricular activities." She paused for a second as Oz raised an eyebrow. "Or . . . my curricular activities," she amended a little dolefully. "Or, you know, the fact of my activeness in general . . ."

* * *

Buffy followed her mother into the hallway outside the cafeteria, hoping the bustle of students would insulate them from anyone having a tendency to pay too close attention to their conversation. Before she could say anything—like point out that talking about murders and monsters in the cafeteria was way low on the desirable list—Joyce slowed to where they could walk side by side. "Are your friends going to help with the investigation, too?"

Buffy hesitated, trying to figure out how best to word this. "Mom, I really think—" She glanced around, deciding that the busy hallway wasn't any better than the busy cafeteria. Way too many prying ears. "Maybe this isn't the best place to talk about this."

Joyce's eyebrows lifted, then she actually had the grace to look self-conscious for her daughter. "Are you embarrassed to be hanging out with your mother? I didn't hug you."

Buffy tried again. "No, it's just . . . this hall is about school." She shrugged. "And you're about home. Mix them, my world dissolves."

"I know. You have no mother, you hatched full-grown out of a giant egg." Joyce managed the tiniest of smiles, but it faded instantly. "It's just . . . I keep thinking about who could have done such a thing. I want to help."

Well, Buffy could certainly understand that—the memory of those children still haunted her, too. "Oh. Well, Giles can always use—"

"I called everybody I know in town," Joyce told her, perking up. "I told them about the dead children. They're all just as upset as I am."

For a moment Buffy was speechless. "You . . . called everybody you know?"

"And they called all *their* friends," Joyce told her

proudly. "And guess what? We're setting up a vigil for tonight at City Hall—the Mayor is even going to be there. *Now* we'll get some action."

Action? Oh boy. "Uh-huh," Buffy said slowly. "That's . . . great. Uh, but, you know what? A lot of times, when we're working on something like this, we like to keep the number of people who know about it kind of . . . small."

"Oh," Joyce said. Obviously this had never occurred to her. "Right. Well, I'm sure there won't be all that many people."

CHAPTER 2

There must have been more than a hundred men and women there.

As she looked around with Buffy, Willow wanted to think this was the result of a "You tell two friends, and they'll tell two friends, and so on, and so on" kind of thing. But there was also the angle of parasitic growth to consider—as in vamps and how they could multiply, if they wanted, with hardly any effort at all. After all, Sunnydale did have a way of taking the innocent and turning it ugly . . . but no, these were just regular people, Sunnydale everydayers—key word *day*—milling around the spacious rotunda at City Hall as they murmured to one another about the terrible crime that had been committed. The air was filled with the faint scent of burning wicks from the unscented candles most of the people carried about like small, personal torches. Those who were candle-deprived had another prize to show off:

signs with enlarged photographs of the two murdered children and the determined slogan "NEVER AGAIN" stretched across the bottom in thick, impossible-to-ignore red letters outlined in black. The same posters, only larger, had been hung all around the rotunda and on the wall behind an oak podium. Everywhere Willow turned, she found the mournful eyes of the child victims staring at her.

"This is great," Buffy said at her side as she eyeballed the crowd. Her voice was heavy with disgust, making no effort at all to hide her displeasure. "Maybe we can *all* go patrolling together later."

"At least your mom's making an effort," Willow pointed out. "My mom's probably—" She faltered as someone edged out of a group and came toward them from among the people milling about. "Standing right in front of me right this second." She stared. "Mom?"

Buffy looked as surprised as she felt when Willow's mother, an exasperated expression on her face, pushed through a final knot of people and joined them. That same astonishment must have been contagious, because it sure showed on Mrs. Rosenberg's face when she saw her daughter. Then her mouth turned up in a pleased smile.

"Willow! I-I didn't know you were going to be here." She glanced at Buffy briefly. "Oh, hi, Bunny."

"Hi," Willow's best friend said, smiling thinly.

"Mom," Willow blurted, "what are you doing here?"

"Oh, well, I read about it in the paper, and what with your dad out of town—" She stopped abruptly, staring at her daughter. "Willow, you cut off your hair! That's a new look."

She tucked a strand behind her ear self-consciously. "Yeah, it's just a sudden whim that I had . . . in August."

The comment was lost on the older woman. "I like it," she said as Buffy's mother joined them. "Hello, Joyce."

"Sheila," Joyce said, much too fondly for Willow's liking. "I'm glad you could come." *You tell two friends, and they'll tell two friends . . .*

"There you are," Giles said as he threaded his way through the crowd. He sounded slightly breathless. "I almost didn't find you in this crush." He started to say something else, then Willow heard his words stutter away as he realized Joyce Summers was standing there. For an awkward moment, the two adults froze as they faced each other, then Giles found a small, strained smile. "Oh, uh, Mrs. . . . . Joyce." He cleared his throat. "This is quite a turnout you've gotten here."

"Well, it's not just me," Mrs. Summers said a little too cheerily. "But thank you." She stared at Giles. "Well," she said again. "It's . . . uh, been a while."

"Right," Giles agreed. "Not since . . . not since . . ." He blinked. "Not for a while."

Willow saw her own mother lean forward. "There's a rumor going around, Mr. Giles."

Oddly, Giles blanched, making Willow wonder what the heck was going on. "A rumor? About us? About what?"

"About witches," Willow's mother said earnestly. "People calling themselves witches are responsible for this brutal crime."

Giles exhaled. "Indeed? How strange."

"Yes," Willow agreed with a nervous laugh. "So strange—witches!" Belatedly she realized how high and anxiety-riddled her voice was. To try to cover, she made a dismissive raspberry sound with her lips.

"Well, actually not that strange," Mrs. Rosenberg put in. She looked at Joyce and Giles and twisted her hands together. "I recently coauthored a paper about the rise of mysticism among adolescents, and I was shocked at the statistical—" She stopped as she noticed activity around the podium. "Oh, are we starting?"

All the people in the overpacked area had finally fallen silent, and Willow and the others turned to look as the Mayor's voice shuddered through the microphone. "Hello, everybody."

Beside her, Mrs. Summers leaned over to Buffy. "He'll do something about this," she told her daughter. "You'll see."

Mayor Wilkins, appropriately attired in a somber gray suit and tie, kept his expression puppy-dog sad and his voice subdued. "I want to thank you all for coming in the aftermath of such a tragic crime," he told the crowd. His gaze swept the room, but Willow could have sworn he was doing that old "look over their heads" trick. Or was that "imagine them all in their underwear"? "Seeing you here proves what a caring community Sunnydale is," Mayor Wilkins continued. "Sure, we've had our share of misfortunes, but we're a *good* town, with *good* people. And I know none of us will rest easy until this horrible murder is solved. With that in mind—" He reached behind the podium and raised one of the signs bearing the photo of the dead children. His voice took on a faintly dramatic tone that Willow found overbearing. "I make these words my pledge to you," Wilkins declared. *"Never again."*

Murmurs of approval and agreement rippled through the crowd, cut here and there by a few overenthusiastics who outright applauded. Wilkins held up his hand. "Now, I ask you to give your attention to the woman who brought us all here tonight, Joyce Summers."

The Mayor gallantly stepped to the side, then guided

Buffy's mother up to the podium. "Thank you," Joyce said, then faced the audience. For a triple beat—stretching long enough to make Willow wonder if Mrs. Summers had been hit with stage fright—the woman didn't make a sound. But when she did speak, her words gave everyone in the audience a jolt. "Mr. Mayor, you're dead wrong."

Uh-oh, Willow thought, and glanced at Buffy. Her friend looked just as surprised as Willow, Giles, and the rest of the people in the room.

At the podium, Joyce Summers's voice cut clearly across the room, and she leaned into the microphone. "This is *not* a good town. How many of us have lost someone who just—just disappeared, or got skinned, or suffered 'neck rupture'? And how many of us have been too afraid to speak out?" Her expression was faintly bewildered as she looked at all of them. "I was supposed to lead us in a moment of silence, but silence is this town's *disease.*"

Next to Willow, Buffy and Giles exchanged worried glances, and Buffy folded her arms in an unconscious gesture of self-protection. "For too long we've been plagued by unnatural evils," Joyce continued. Her voice was growing stronger. "This isn't our town anymore. It belongs to the monsters and the witches, and the Slayers."

Willow gasped and saw Buffy's eyes widen, then shadow over with hurt. And no wonder. How could her friend's mother say such a thing—didn't she realize that by doing so she was lumping the town's salvation, its source of *good,* in with all the bad?

At the podium, Mrs. Summers now stood straight and tall, and her tone was filled with determination as she gripped the sides of the wooden stand. "I say it's time for the grown-ups to take Sunnydale *back*. And I say we start by finding the people who did this and making them *pay*."

Shocked, all Willow could do was stand there with Buffy and Giles and watch as everyone in the audience—including her own mother—cheered and heartily applauded Joyce Summers's declaration of retaliation.

Hours had passed.

Sunnydale lay mostly in slumber, with only a few lit windows to break the quiet darkness. They had the candles all lit—mostly black and red, incense, the human skull with the hole drilled in the top. The cauldron was ready, filled with the appropriate mixture of herbs and other lesser-known ingredients.

Sitting on the floor, a teenager named Michael leaned forward and adjusted something within the carefully arranged, oversized altar on the floor before them. His face was moon-white beneath a black hood, and his eyes, outlined in kohl, looked deep-set and dark above lips that were painted as black as the fabric draped over his head and his ink-colored hair.

Amy stood a few feet away, her deep auburn hair framing her pretty face and adding to the shadows cast by her own black hood. Without speaking, she bent over and carefully poured the powdered concoction she held in her palm into the hole in the top of the skull, then picked up the skull and stood. When she took a couple of steps forward and sat, she became one corner of a human triangle in the center of which, in sweeping white strokes against black, was a huge rendition of the same symbol that had been drawn on the palms of the two murdered children. The third person in the group took a place at the symbol's triangular apex, then added a portion of black and red powders to the mixture already in the small cauldron. After a moment of meditation by all three, she leaned forward and carefully set the contents on fire, watching as heavy red smoke billowed around them and into the familiar room—Willow's.

With her bright red hair shrouded by a heavy hood, Willow was barely recognizable.

CHAPTER 3

Buffy saw it start to happen from halfway down the hall, and her keen hearing picked up every word even as she lengthened her stride and began to weave through the mass of students hurrying in every direction.

She hadn't known him long, but Michael was an okay guy, maybe a little on the small side considering he had a penchant for going Goth, and that could attract all kinds of wrong attention. As he opened his locker and checked out his appearance—decked out in full tortured-soul mode, blackened lips included—in a stick-up mirror, he didn't see the knot of jock-jerks until they were right in front of his locker. As he stepped away from the door, Michael jumped as the lead one, Roy, reached out and slammed it, just missing his nose.

"Watch it!" Michael exclaimed.

In response the bigger guy grabbed Michael's collar and bounced him backward against the metal. "Oh, sorry."

Roy sneered. "Did I make you smudge your eyeliner? Gonna put a spell on me?"

Amy, getting something from her own locker a few feet away, stepped forward. "Hey, what is your problem?"

Hammy fists still wrapped firmly in Michael's collar, Roy looked over at her, then shoved his face close to Michael's. His cronies huddled close for support. "Everyone knows he's into that voodoo witch crap. I heard about those kids—people like him gotta learn a lesson."

"And what about people like me?" Amy demanded hotly.

He gave her a withering glance. "Get in my face and you'll find out."

A small crowd of students had already gathered, and Buffy gave silent thanks that she'd only been half the hallway's length away. This was happening so quickly— had she been way over by the main entrance, poor Michael would have been pummeled by now. Whatever might have been, however, quickly dissipated when she angled past the last two or three teenagers and, making sure she was wearing the cheerfulest of expectant smiles, leaned her head in between Amy and Roy.

Healthy and athletic, Roy still stopped dead when he saw her. "Uh . . . no problem here." His big hands loosened, then he gave Michael's rumpled shirt a small pat and tug to put it back in place. He glanced at her again, then nodded to his pals. "We're walking."

The three of them watched the group take off, then Buffy turned back to Amy and Michael. "You guys okay?"

"Yeah," Michael said. He sounded totally disgusted. "We're fine."

"Thanks, Buffy," Amy added. She and Michael walked away, and Buffy saw Michael rub his arm where his elbow had hit the lockers. Again, it was a good thing she'd been around. Even Giles had been drawn out of the library by the noise of the potential fight, and his expression clearly indicated he wanted to speak with her. As she started to go to him, the sound of Cordelia's voice made her realize that her Watcher wasn't the only one waiting for her time and attention.

"You're going to be one busy little Slayer, baby-sitting them."

Buffy regarded her. "I doubt they'll have any more trouble."

Cordelia's face remained calm and expressionless, almost cold. "I doubt your doubt. Everyone knows that witches killed those kids, and Amy is a witch. And Michael is . . . whatever a boy witch is, plus being the poster child for yuck."

"Cordelia—"

The dark-haired girl hugged her books. "If you're going to hang with them," she said icily, "expect badness. Because that's what you get when you hang with freaks and losers. Believe me, I *know*." She spun, but before she'd taken five steps, she turned back briefly and raised an eyebrow. "That was a pointed comment about me hanging with you guys."

"Yeah, I got that one," Buffy said, but Cordelia's back was to her, and she was already striding away. "Besides," she called a little angrily, "witches didn't *do* it!"

Behind her, Buffy heard Giles clear his throat. When she faced him, he leaned closer, his voice dropping confidentially. "Actually, I think they may have. My research keeps leading me back to European Wiccan covens."

"You found the meaning of the symbol?"

"I'm pretty sure, yes." Despite his words, he seemed anything but. "There's a piece of information that I need that's in a book Willow borrowed. Can you find it?"

"No problem," she said.

* * *

The first moment she had, Buffy headed for the student lounge. Inside, it was easy to pick out Xander slouched on one of the couches.

"Buffy," he said brightly. "Hi."

"Hey," she said. "Is Willow around?"

Xander scowled defensively and sat up straighter. "How can I convince you people that it's over? You assume because I'm here, she's here—that I somehow, mysteriously, know where she is."

Buffy glanced at a table a few feet away and saw a couple of books, the edge of a familiar notebook. "Are those hers?"

"Yeah," Xander answered. "She's in the bathroom."

Buffy didn't say anything, just went over and started looking through the books.

Trailing after her, Xander was working himself into full indignation zone. "But the fact that I know that doesn't change that I have a genuine complaint here," he insisted. "Look, I'm sick of the judgment, the innuendo. Is a man not innocent until proven guilty?"

There, second from the top, was undoubtedly the one Giles was looking for—the nasty symbol etched into its cover was hard to miss. "You *are* guilty," she told him without missing a beat. "You got illicit smoochies, you have to pay the price."

"But I'm talking about *future* guilt." Xander waved his arm at the room in general. "Everyone expects me to mess up again. Like Oz—I see the way he is around me. You know, that steely gaze, the pointed silence."

"Because he's usually such a chatterbox." Buffy flipped through the book, but it was mostly text. Some heavy reading here.

"No," Xander protested. "It's different now. It's more a *verbal* nonverbal. He says volumes with his eyes."

Buffy started to respond, then stopped as her gaze went

to the table and Willow's open notebook. She managed not to recoil, but just barely.

She couldn't believe what she was seeing. There, on a page in the center of her best friend's notebook, was *the* symbol, that very *same* symbol, hand-copied with a big black marker and surrounded by her friend's neatly written notes.

It matched exactly with what had been drawn on the palms of the murdered kids.

Buffy was standing by her pile of books when Willow came out of the restroom. "Hey, Buff," she said. "Whatcha looking for—you want to borrow something?"

Her friend picked up Willow's notebook by its edges, as though she were unwilling to touch it. "What's . . . this?" she asked.

There was something wrong here, big-time. Willow could hear it in Buffy's voice, see it in the tenseness of her shoulders, read it in the hard way her friend's eyes looked more Slayer than schoolmate. She looked at Buffy, then at the notebook. "A doodle," she said nervously. "I do doodle. You, too—you do doodle, too."

Xander folded his arms and gazed at Buffy. "You're not going to make me feel better, are you?" He sounded completely exasperated.

Willow didn't know what he was talking about, but Buffy ignored him and faced her. "This is a witch symbol."

Confused, Willow could only nod. "Okay, yeah. It is."

"Willow!"

"*What?*"

Buffy pointed to the symbol. "That symbol was on the murdered children!"

For a long second, Willow simply stared at her, unable to process what she'd just heard. When she did speak, her words were jumbled and running into one another. Dread seeped into her arms and legs, making her weak. "It was on the kids . . . oh, no, Buffy—I didn't know, no one told me about that. I swear—"

Before she could finish, there was a huge commotion in the hallway outside the lounge, with people yelling and banging, a whole bunch of locker doors clanging open and against one another. Her attention momentarily diverted, Buffy handed Willow her notebook and watched as she gathered the rest of her stuff. Then the three of them hurried to the hallway to see what was what. Just as they got there, a voice echoed over a bullhorn farther down the hall.

"Stay away from the lockers—this is police business! Stay away!"

Students were smashed together in the hallway, trying to get closer to their lockers despite the warnings. Teachers wandered among them, their faces grim and etched with determination, without a hint of mercy or sympathy. Principal Snyder appeared absurdly pleased as he paced along the rows of lockers, supervising a custodian who bypassed the combination locks with a master key. Armed security guards flanked the custodian, their eyes mistrustful as they gazed at the unhappy students. Farther down, Buffy saw another faculty member stopping students and rudely searching through their purses and backpacks. As she, Willow, and Xander stared in dismay, Oz and Amy joined them. A few feet away, Willow saw an outraged Cordelia, no doubt mentally preparing herself for a tirade.

"Oh, man," Xander said beneath his breath. "It's Nazi Germany, and I've got *Playboys* in my locker."

Ten yards away, the ratty, exhilarated smile on Snyder's face was impossible to miss. "This is a glorious day for principals everywhere!" he declared loudly. "No pathetic whining about students' rights—just a long row of lockers and a man with a key."

Oz leaned in between Buffy and Willow, keeping his voice low. "They just took three kids away," he told them.

Buffy frowned. "What are they looking for?"

Amy slid close to them, her face pale and distressed. "Witch stuff."

Willow gaped at her. "What?"

"They got my spells," Amy said in a low voice. "I'm supposed to report to Snyder's office."

"Oh, my God," Willow whispered.

She tried to think of something comforting to say to Amy, but the thought was lost when a teacher stepped out of the crowd and took Amy by the arm. "Okay, Amy," he said gruffly. "You'll have to come with me."

Amy didn't bother resisting as he led her away, but she did look back over her shoulder. "Willow, be *careful*."

Panic threatened to overwhelm Willow, and she turned back to Buffy. "I have stuff in my locker!" She looked around a little wildly as more lockers were forced open. "Henbane, hellibore, mandrake root—"

"Excuse me," Xander interrupted, and Willow could have just shaken him. "*Playboys?* Can we work the sympathy this-a-way?"

Buffy looked as if she was going to retort, then there was a bang as another locker was opened. Cordelia's sharp voice rose above the unhappy muttering of the students. "Hey! Get your grubby custodial hands *off* that! That hair spray cost forty-five dollars *and* it's imported!"

We all have our priorities, Willow thought a little dizzily. She touched Buffy's arm, still unable to believe what was happening. "My locker's next—Buffy, I didn't do anything *wrong*. That symbol . . . it's harmless. I used it to make a protection spell for you, for your birthday, with Michael and Amy. Only now it's broken, because you know about it, and so happy birthday, and *please*— you have to believe me!"

She could almost *feel* Snyder going through her locker, putting his weasely little fingers all over her personal belongings. It was only a matter of seconds—

"Ms. Rosenberg," the principal said in a calm, disgustingly delighted voice as he held up two bags of dried herbs and roots. "My office."

Convinced she was doomed, she looked at the floor and started toward where Snyder waited. Her heart was pounding with terror—what was she going to do? She faltered a little as Buffy suddenly cut across her path, then felt a welcome bit of relief as her friend oh-so-casually lifted her notebook and Giles's witchcraft book from her arms without anyone noticing. To help her even more, Oz immediately fell in step next to her.

She hoped he wasn't just following her along the path to damnation . . .

Buffy burst through the library doors, thinking that she was leaving the chaos of modern-day search and seizure behind.

She was wrong.

Three steps in, and an armed guard, a clone of the ones out by the students' lockers, pushed past her all the while juggling a full box of library books. She glared at him, then realized there were others inside and up the stairs, even inside the library cage, piling more of Giles's books haphazardly into a dozen waiting boxes. A good portion of the library was in disarray, and Giles was so angry he was practically sputtering. "Giles?"

The librarian hurried up to her, then spread his hands. "They're confiscating my books!"

41

He joined her at the counter. "Giles, we *need* those books."

"Believe me," Giles said, and grimaced at one of the guards. "I tried telling that to the nice man with the big gun."

"No," she said. She stepped closer, trying to make him understand and keep her voice down at the same time. "There's something about this symbol we're not getting— Willow said she used it in a *protection* spell. It's harmless, not a big bad, so why would it turn up in a ritual sacrifice?"

"I don't know," Giles admitted. Frustration put lines in his forehead. "Ordinarily I would say let's widen our research—"

"With what?" Buffy demanded. "A dictionary and *My Friend Flicka?*"

Giles spun, becoming more furious as another box of books was hauled away. "This is *intolerable*," he growled as Buffy set Willow's notebook and the book she'd retrieved on the counter. "Snyder has interfered before, but I won't take *this* from that twisted little homunculus!"

Before Buffy's Watcher could continue his tirade, Snyder's sharp voice cut the air from a few feet away. "I love the smell of desperate librarian in the morning," he said smugly. He toasted Giles with his coffee cup as yet another guard hurried past and began rummaging along the library shelves.

Every muscle in Giles's face was rigid, and he looked as if the only thing in the world he wanted was to pop the principal in the nose. "Get out," Giles said between clenched teeth. "And take your . . . your *marauders* with you."

"Oh, my. So fierce." Snyder glanced around the library. "I suppose I should hear you out," he said, then reached over and plucked a book from the top of a pile waiting to be packed up. "Tell me, just how is, um, *Blood Rites and Sacrifices* appropriate material for a public school library? Is the Chess Club branching out?" He tossed the book into an open box, not noticing as Buffy casually reached out and pushed Willow's items off the counter. Amid the racket made by the guards, no one noticed the sound they made as they fell out of sight.

"Those items are my personal research materials," Giles said hotly. "I assure you, they're all perfectly harmless."

The words had barely left his mouth when a guard inside the library cage noticed the cabinet door and pulled it open. Buffy winced as the uniformed man turned to Snyder and gestured to get his attention. Snyder glanced at the weaponry displayed inside—their deadly collection of crossbows, axes, spears, and more—then turned back toward Giles and grinned gleefully. "And?"

"They're antiques," Giles said quickly.

"And so are you," Snyder shot back. "A relic of a progressive era that is finally coming to an end. Welcome to the *new* new age." He tipped the coffee cup toward them and started to walk away.

"This is *not* over," Giles snarled.

Snyder stopped. "Oh, I'd say it's just beginning. Fight it if you want. Just remember—lift a finger against me, and you'll have to answer to MOO."

Buffy could stand it no longer. "MOO? Did that sentence make some sense that I'm just not in on?"

" 'Mothers Opposed to the Occult,' " Snyder said briskly.

Buffy rolled her eyes. "And who came up with *that* lame name?"

Snyder took a sip of his coffee, then stepped past Buffy and Giles. "That would be the founder," he said haughtily as he strolled away. "I believe you call her Mom."

CHAPTER 4

It seemed that today's surprises weren't over yet.

Willow found her mother waiting for her when she got home. Sheila Rosenberg was sitting in front of the coffee table, upon which was spread the entirety of the magic-making items that had been confiscated from Willow's locker at school. There was a whole array of some of her best things—plastic bags of finely ground roots and hard-to-find herbs, charms, and various rocks that she had blessed along the line. When she came into the living room, she found her mother holding up a tiny dried white corncob charm and peering at it curiously. "Oooh," Sheila said when she realized her daughter was standing there. "Sit down, honey."

Timidly, Willow settled on the love seat across from her mother, with the coffee table between them. "Principal Snyder talked to you?"

Sheila nodded. "Yes. He's quite concerned."

Willow leaned forward. "Mom, I know what it looks like, but I can totally—"

Sheila waved a hand, cutting off Willow's words. "You don't have to explain, honey. This isn't exactly a surprise."

Willow squinted at her. "Why . . . not?"

Sheila folded her hands in her lap and looked at Willow calmly. "Oh, well, identification with mythical icons is perfectly typical of your age group. It's a . . . a classic adolescent response to the pressure of incipient adulthood."

"Oh," Willow said, disappointed. "Is that what it is?"

Her mother nodded, then looked at the items on the coffee table distastefully. "Of course, I wish you would have identified with something a little less icky, but developmentally speaking—"

"Mom, I'm not in an age group," Willow interrupted. She twisted her fingers. "I'm *me*. Willow group."

Sheila stood and came over to sit next to her. "I understand—"

"No, you don't," Willow said, a little desperately. "Mom, this may be hard for you to accept, but I can . . . do stuff. Nothing bad or dangerous, but I can do spells—"

"You *think* you can," her mother said firmly. "And that's what concerns me. The delusions—"

Frustration made Willow exhale. "Mom, I mean, how would you know *what* I can do? The last time we had a conversation over three minutes, it was about the patriarchal bias of the *Mr. Rogers* show."

"Well," Sheila said indignantly. She sat back and made quote-mark gestures in the air with her hands. "With King Friday lording it over all the lesser puppets—"

"Mom, you're not paying attention!"

Sheila patted her on the knee and let her voice take on a soothing tone. "And this is your way of trying to get it. Now, I've consulted with some of my colleagues, and they agree that this is a cry for discipline." She paused. "You're grounded."

Willow's mouth fell open. *"Grounded?* This is the first time, *ever,* I've done something you don't like, and I'm grounded? I'm *supposed* to mess up—I'm a teenager, remember?"

Sheila nodded agreeably. "You're upset. I hear you."

Willow felt her face flush with anger and jumped to her feet. "No, Ma—hear *this.* I'm a rebel! I'm having a rebellion—"

The older woman looked at her with exaggerated patience. "Willow, honey, you don't have to act out like this to prove your specialness."

But the condescending expression just made Willow more irate. "Mom, I'm not acting out—I'm a *witch.* I can make pencils float, and I can summon the four elements—well, two elements, but four soon." She paused, searching for something, anything, that would have an impact. "And—and I'm dating a musician!"

"Oh, Willow!"

Willow couldn't believe that was the only thing that had gotten through—what about the rest of it, her desires, interests, her Wiccan talents, her *personality,* for crying out loud? Anger at her mother hit her in a rush and hurt deeper than anything her mom had ever made her feel before. "I worship Beelzebub!" she announced loudly. "I do his bidding—do you see any goats around? No, because I sacrificed them all!"

"Will, please." Finally, some reaction—the parental unit was at least becoming unstuck.

"All bow before Satan!"

Sheila stood abruptly, her face creased in aggravation. "I'm not listening to this."

She started to stalk out of the room, but Willow was on

a roll. She followed, determined to find a spot in her mother's brain somewhere that would make her realize her daughter existed in the world as a unique person, an individual who couldn't be categorized by statistics and university papers and psychology. "Prince of Night, I summon you!" she called, raising her face to the ceiling. "Come fill me with your black, naughty evil!"

"That's *enough!*" Sheila yelled.

Oops, Willow thought belatedly. *Guess I found that nerve.*

The older woman's face was rigid and furious. "Now, you will go to your room and stay there until I say otherwise," she said in a don't-even-think-about-arguing voice. "And we're going to make some changes—I don't want you hanging out with those friends of yours. It's clear where this little obsession came from."

Her final decree as she ushered Willow up the stairs to her room was as shocking as it was sharp.

"You will not speak to Bunny Summers again."

"I don't want you seeing that Willow anymore," Joyce Summers said. "I've spoken with her mother—I had no idea her forays into the occult had gone so far."

Speechless, all Buffy could do was stare at Joyce. She felt as if she'd stepped out of sync with time for a month or two, and while she was gone her mother, and most of the town, had gone crazy. The insanity had even come to roost inside her house, where somehow her mom had converted a perfectly normal dining room into an area that was half bizarre campaign office and half morbid shrine. On the table that was now a desk was her mother's laptop computer, but it was almost lost in the phone lists, file folders, papers, pamphlets, and paraphernalia. The sorrowful eyes of the murdered little boy and girl watched her from posters in every corner of the room; more signs leaned against the desk and all available wall space. Red buttons—"MOO, Mothers Opposed to the Occult!"—littered the space around the computer, and, of course, one was pinned to her mother's lapel.

"You're the one who ordered the raid on the school today," Buffy said in amazement.

Joyce gave her a dismissive glance. "Honey, they opened a few lockers."

"Lockers," Buffy said pointedly. Her words got more frantic. "First syllable, *lock.* They're supposed to be private, and they took all of Giles's books away!"

"He'll get most of them back," her mother said as she made a notation on some form or another. "MOO just wants to weed out the offensive material. Everything else will be returned to Mr. Giles soon."

Annoyed, Buffy paced in front of the table. "If we're going to solve this, we need those books *now.*"

"Sweetie, those books had no place in a public school library. Any student can waltz in there and get all sorts of ideas." Joyce stood and came around the table, stopping in front of Buffy with her fists clenched. "Do you understand how that terrifies me?"

Buffy pressed her lips together, trying to be patient, needing, *willing,* her mother to see her point of view. "Mom, I hate that these people scared you so much. And I—I know you're trying to help. But you have to let *me* handle this. It's what I *do.*"

Her mother only looked at her placidly. "But is it really? I mean, you patrol. You slay. Evil pops up, you undo it. And that's great—but is Sunnydale getting any better? Are they running out of vampires?"

"I don't think they run out—"

"It's not your fault," Joyce said gently. "You don't have

a plan. You just react to things. It's bound to be kind of . . . fruitless."

Buffy took a step backward, stung, then turned in a circle as she tried to organize her thoughts. After a moment, she said, "Okay, maybe I don't have a *plan*. Lord knows I don't have lapel buttons—"

"Buffy—"

"—and maybe the next time the world is getting sucked into Hell, I won't be able to stop it, because the anti-Hell-sucking book isn't on the approved reading list!" She glared at Joyce.

"I'm sorry," Joyce said. "I didn't mean to put down—"

"Yeah, well, you did," Buffy cut in, then shook her head. "It doesn't matter. I have to go—I have to go on one of my pointless patrols and 'react' to some vampires . . . *if* that's all right with MOO."

Joyce didn't say anything, just stood there watching her. Buffy couldn't help stopping on her way out and sending her mother a final, disgusted glance. "And nice acronym, Mom!"

Joyce sighed, feeling the weariness caused by this terrible situation all the way down to her bones. "I'm just trying to make things better," she said to herself softly.

"You are."

She turned slowly to her right and saw . . . *them,* just as she had a dozen or more times since the night she'd found them on the merry-go-round in the park. This time they were sitting on the chairs she'd placed on the other side of the table, their small feet not even close to touching the floor, their ashen faces sad and beseeching, filled with the regret of two lifetimes they would never experience. Their bluish lips hardly moved when they spoke, and

Joyce had to lean in close to hear their semi-whispered words.

"There's bad people out there," the little girl said. She seemed even tinier on the big chair, her child's overalls loose over her striped shirt.

"And we can't sleep," the boy added.

The girl's eyes seemed to pin Joyce down, to paralyze her where she stood. *"Not until you hurt them,"* she whispered.

The boy nodded ever so slightly. *"The way they hurt us . . ."*

CHAPTER 5

Tonight the playground was eerily quiet.

No bushes rustled, no leaves blew across the walkway, not even a breeze dared to shake the overhead branches of the trees. The vampires and beasties of the night had elected to stay huddled away from the child murderer that apparently still roamed free on the streets of Sunnydale . . . or perhaps they *and* the murderer were hiding from the fever that had gripped the town in the wake of the gruesome killings.

Foreboding scratched at Buffy as she patrolled the park, although it had nothing to do with bloodsuckers, stakes, and holy water. Something about Sunnydale was *off*, skewed in a way she'd never before encountered. She couldn't put a name to the sensation, but she knew it was wrong . . . and she didn't know how to fight it.

And ahead was the hard proof of it.

Innocent on the surface, the sight that met Buffy's eyes

was indicative of emotions gone to the extreme. The merry-go-round and the ground next to it where her mother had discovered the children was now blanketed in red and blue candles, cards, and photographs. Between the pictures and spots of softly glowing flame were bowls and vases of flowers, so many that it looked like an outdoor version of a funeral home waking room. As she walked slowly toward the piece of playground equipment turned shrine, from the corner of her eye Buffy saw Angel slip into step beside her.

"Hey," he said.

She stopped and faced him, welcomed the comfort of his embrace as he hugged her. "Hey," she said softly. She ran her fingers along one of his sleeves. "How are you?"

"I'm all right." He studied her, his face solemn. "I think I'm better than you right now."

Buffy pulled out of his arms and faced the improvised memorial, then looked glumly at the ground. He was so close to the truth that she didn't know what to say.

"I heard about this," Angel said in a low voice as he eyed the merry-go-round. "People are talking. People are even talking to me."

"It's strange," she said. Her voice sounded hollow in the emptiness out here, as though it had a slight echo at the edge. "People die in Sunnydale all the time. But I've never seen anything like this."

When she turned and headed for the park bench at the border of the playground, Angel followed. "They were children—innocent. It makes a difference."

"And Mr. Sanderson from the bank had it coming?" Buffy sat, still staring at the shrine, thinking how it looked like a little island of glowing light in the midst of darkness. "My mom," she said slowly, "said some things to me about being the Slayer. That it's fruitless." She looked at her fingers, then raised her gaze to his and shook her head. "No fruit for Buffy."

"She's wrong."

"Is she?" Buffy searched Angel's eyes. "*Is* Sunnydale any better than when I first came here? Okay, so I battle evil . . . but I don't really win. The bad keeps coming back and getting *stronger.* I'm like the kid in that story, the boy who stuck his finger in the duck."

Angel blinked. "Dike." When she only looked confused, he explained. "It's another word for dam."

"Oh," she said. "Okay, that story makes a lot more sense now."

Angel took her hand. "Buffy, you know I'm still figuring things out. There's a lot I don't understand. But I do know it's important to keep fighting. And I learned that from you."

"But we never—"

"We never win," he finished for her.

Buffy looked at him sadly. "Not completely."

"We never will." He squeezed her fingers. "That's not why we fight. We do it because there are things worth fighting *for.*" She remained silent, and he looked toward the playground area again, the telling circle of candles, photographs, and flowers. "Those kids. Their parents."

Yeah, Buffy thought. *Of course. Their*— She sat up a little straighter. "Their parents . . ."

"Look," Angel said, "I know it's not much—"

"No," Buffy replied. Her thoughts were churning as she tried to make sense of a few things that had suddenly crashed into each other in her brain. "No, it's a *lot.*"

When Oz and Xander strode into the library, the first thing Oz noticed were the huge, ugly gaps in the bookshelves, sad evidence that the heart had been cut out of most of the Watcher realm of Giles's world.

The second thing the two teenagers saw was Giles himself.

The librarian looked totally out of place, sitting at the library table in front of the computer for which he had never hidden his dislike. He was leaning toward it with a small bag of munchies—probably something dry and tastelessly adult—clutched in his right hand while he poked angrily at the keyboard with his left. In the time it took for Oz and Xander to walk through the door and past the counter, Giles had already made several rude gestures at the screen and gone into shouting mode.

"Session interrupted?" Giles's voice rose even louder as he stared at the monitor in amazement, then jammed another tidbit from his bag into his mouth and chewed furiously. "Who said you could interrupt, you stupid, *useless* fad! That's right—I said *fad!* And I'll say it again!"

"At that point I will become frightened," Xander said next to him.

"Take heart," Oz said. "We found your books." At the almost painfully grateful expression on Giles's face when he turned and looked at them, Oz wished then that he hadn't made such an announcement of it.

"You can put the heart back," Xander said quickly. "We can't get 'em—they're locked up in City Hall." He leaned over Giles's shoulder, trying to read what was on the computer screen. " 'Frisky Watchers Chat Room.' Why, Giles . . ."

Giles shot Xander a withering look, but before the librarian could retort, Buffy burst into the library. "Buffy!" Xander exclaimed. "Oz and I found out—"

"What do we know about those kids?" she interrupted. Giles frowned. "What?"

"Facts," Buffy said sharply. "Details."

"Well, they were found in the park," Xander began.

Buffy held up a hand, stopping him. "No—where did they go to school? Who are their parents? What are their *names?*"

Oz looked at Giles and Xander, but none of them had any answers. At their perplexed expressions, Buffy continued. "We know everything about their deaths, but we don't even know their *names!*"

"Sure we do," Xander offered. Then he hesitated. "Uh . . . it's on the tip of my tongue—"

Oz pondered this. "It never came up. Ever."

Buffy nodded. "And if no one knows who they are, where did these pictures come from?"

Giles sat back. "I—I just assumed that someone had the details. I never really . . . well, it is strange."

Buffy jerked a finger at the computer. "We need to get some information."

"Well, let somebody else do it," Giles said in indignation. He glared at the computer. "This thing has locked me out."

Xander grinned. "Well, if you wouldn't yell at it . . ."

Oz stepped up to the table, and Giles gave him a thankful nod and pushed himself out of the chair, offering it. "I can look around," Oz said, and settled in front of the keyboard. "But Willow would really know the sites we need."

"That's great," Buffy said. She was practically spinning in frustration. "She can't even come to the phone."

Oz smiled a little as he covered the mouse with his fingers. "We don't need the phone." The cursor zipped around the screen as he found the dial-up program and keyed in Willow's modem line. A few seconds later, a pop-up menu indicated she'd picked up the call on her computer. "All right," Oz said. "We're linked. If anybody ID'd the kids, she'll pull it up and feed it here."

Willow had been lying on her bed, aimlessly bouncing her teddy bear up and down while she tried to figure out some way to reach her mother and make her understand that she wasn't losing her mind or anything ridiculous like that. Like so many adults, her mom had immediately discounted the supernatural, and where would they be in Sunnydale if, for instance, Buffy had done that back when she'd first transferred here? Willow didn't have a working crystal ball—yet—but she didn't think she needed one to know they'd all be neck deep, pun intended, in a world of hurt and deep evil if the Slayer had pooh-poohed the concept of bloodsuckers and chalked Giles up as being no more than a nutty old bookworm.

The beep of the computer had given her a welcome distraction, and she'd even more appreciated being able to pitch in and help with the gang's activities, if only via remote. It really was amazing, she realized as she read Oz's message and request, that no one had questioned the history of the kids before now. All those photographs . . . they were all depictions of the boy and girl standing together, staring into the camera with melancholy expressions and open, very much *alive* eyes—since when were murder victims able to pose like that?

It didn't take long, maybe three minutes, for her to hit several of her favorite research sites and start coming up with the info. When the first of the newspaper articles appeared, she scanned it with interest and hit the SEND button so her pals at the library could read it, too, even before the accompanying photograph was fully loaded.

* * *

Oz motioned at Giles and the others, and they crowded around behind him to get a look at the monitor.

"Two children," Giles read, "found dead. Mysterious mark . . . no. These children were found near Omaha in 1949."

Xander made a dismissive noise. "They ain't ours. Keep going."

Oz reached for the forward arrow, but Buffy stopped him. "Wait."

He paused and focused on the black-and-white image downloading on the screen, the resolution improving with each passing second. Soon the image was obviously of two little kids, and when it was finally finished and sharp, the four of them stared at it.

"The same kids," Buffy said.

Giles's voice was filled with amazement. "More than fifty years ago!"

Off-site, Willow must have found something else, because suddenly the screen's contents shifted and a new article, this one without a photograph, took the place of the previous information.

Oz leaned forward to read it. "Utah, 1899, two children—rural community torn apart by suspicion."

"A hundred years," Giles said, perplexed. "Yes, but how is that possible?"

Oz kept reading. "There's no mention of who they were."

Buffy crossed her arms. "They've never been seen alive, just dead. A *lot*."

The screen image wiped again, this time filling with old-style German type. In the upper right of the article was a reproduction of an antique woodcut; not very well rendered, yet the two small figures on it were still eerily familiar. A message box flashed in the upper right of the screen, and Oz read aloud what Willow had noted in it. "Yeah, there are more articles. Every fifty years, all the same."

"From as far back as 1649," Giles said thoughtfully. "May I see that?"

Oz rose and let the librarian take his place in front of the computer, watching as Giles scrolled down and concentrated on translating the German. "Written by a cleric from a village near the Black Forest," the Watcher told them. "He found the bodies himself, two children, Greta Strauss, age six, and Hans Strauss, age eight."

"So they have names," Xander murmured. "That's new."

The computer bleeped, and Giles stared at it in confusion. "What—"

Oz reached over his shoulder and tapped a key. "We lost Willow."

Leaning on her elbows as she read from the screen, Willow jumped when her mother opened her door wide and strode over to the bed. "I thought I made myself clear," Sheila Rosenberg said angrily. "You're not minding me, Willow." Before Willow could think, the older woman reached down and closed the laptop, then her fingers slid to the side and disconnected the modem line. She lifted it from the bed and tucked it under her arm. "I see what you're doing," Sheila said. "You're challenging me. But I will *not* have you communicating with your . . . cyber-coven or what have you."

Willow brought her legs around and sat upright. "Coven? What happened to me being delusional and acting out?"

Sheila hesitated, and when she spoke again, some of the sternness of her voice had vanished. "Well, that was before I talked in depth with Ms. Summers and her associates. It seems I've been rather close-minded." She waved a hand in the air.

Willow brightened. "So—you believe me?"

Her mother's face softened, and she smiled sweetly. "I believe you, dear." She hesitated again for the briefest of moments, then said, "Now all I can do is let you go with love."

Willow's mouth dropped open. "Let me go? What does that mean? Mom?"

Her mother didn't answer. Instead she turned and walked out of Willow's room, shut the door behind herself—

—and locked it.

CHAPTER 6

"I can't get her back—she's gone off-line," Oz told them. He tried again, but it was no use.

"No, wait a minute," Giles said as he paced around the room. "Greta Strauss, Hans Strauss." After a few seconds, he hurried over to a bookshelf, then realized the books he so desperately wanted were gone. He looked at the empty spaces helplessly, then turned back to Oz and the others, trying to pull the facts from his overtaxed memory. "There is a fringe theory held by a few folklorists that some regional stories have actual, very *literal* antecedents," he said. He pulled off his glasses and chewed absently on one earpiece.

Buffy's mouth turned down. "And in some language that's English?"

Oz gave up on trying to reconnect with Willow and looked over at Giles. "Fairy tales are real."

"Ah. Hans and Greta." Her brow furrowed as she

crossed her arms and tried to work this out. "Hansel and Gretel?"

"Wait," Xander protested. *"Hansel and Gretel?* As in breadcrumbs, ovens, gingerbread house?"

"Of course," Giles said distractedly. "It makes sense now."

Buffy frowned. "Yeah, it's all falling into place. Of course, *that* place is nowhere near *this* place."

"There are demons that thrive by fostering persecution and hatred among the mortal animals," Giles explained. "Not by destroying men but by watching them destroy each other. They feed us our darkest fear and, by doing so, turn peaceful communities into vigilantes."

Understanding slipped over Buffy's features. "Hansel and Gretel run home to tell everyone about the mean old witch—"

"And she and probably dozens of others are punished by a righteous mob," Giles finished. "It's happened throughout history—it happened in Salem, not surprisingly."

Xander blinked. "Whoa, whoa, whoa—I'm still spinning on the whole fairy-tales-are-real thing."

"What do we do?" Oz asked as Giles paced in front of him again.

"I don't know about you," Xander put in glibly, "but I'm going to go trade my cow for some beans." When they glared at him, he hunched up his shoulders. "No one else is seeing the funny here?"

"Giles," Buffy said in a rush, "we need to talk to Mom. If she knows the truth, she can defuse this whole thing—"

Before she could keep going, the library door burst open and Michael barreled through. His face was bloodied and full of bruises, and Oz and the others ran to him as he clutched at the counter.

Xander was the quickest on the verbal draw list. "What happened?"

Michael gasped for breath, finally found enough to push out the words. "I was attacked!"

Xander winced. "Officially not funny."

"By whom?" Buffy demanded.

Michael hugged himself and struggled for more air, his expression full of a pain that had nothing to do with the physical. "My *dad!* His friends. They're taking people out of their homes, something about a trial down at City Hall—" He inhaled harshly. "They've got Amy."

Oz jerked. "Willow!"

Michael reached out and clutched at Oz's arm. "Tell her to get out of her house!"

"Michael, stay here and hide," Buffy instructed.

"In my office," Giles added.

"Giles, we'll go find my mom." Buffy turned toward Oz. "Oz, you and Xander—"

But Oz was already at the library door, with Xander right behind him. "We're already gone."

Wow, being stuck in here like this just bites, Willow thought.

She'd been lying on the bed with the teddy bear since her mom had barged in and pulled the plug on the computer. There was plenty of stuff she could do, of course—for a start, she could pick up one of a hundred of her favorite books. There were also a couple of extracurricular projects she'd been wanting to start.

She heard a click as her bedroom door unlocked, and Willow was on her feet and headed for it instantly. "Mom," she began, "we have to talk—"

The sight of her mother standing with three other strangers, two men and a woman, stunned her into momentary silence. Unfriendly faces on all except her mom, and what was that pinned to the collars of everyone? Mrs. Summers's ridiculous MOO buttons, of course.

"It's time to go," Sheila said matter-of-factly. "And get your coat—it's chilly out." She stood there, waiting.

Bewildered, Willow didn't react right away. "G-go? Go where—"

Her mother's voice went shockingly harsh. "I said get your coat, *witch!*"

There was no time to think about what she should do. Instinctively, Willow lunged forward and slammed the door shut in her mother's face, then struggled desperately to hold it there as the pounding and shouting began on the other side . . .

Buffy could smell cookies and baked hors d'oeuvres when she and Giles rushed through the front door into her house. It was an absurdly *homey* smell, one that, for just a second, made her think this entire situation had been a mistake that had somehow rectified itself in the time it had taken her and her Watcher to get from the library to here.

But when she turned into the living room, she immediately saw how wrong an idea that was.

Her mother was sitting on a chair she'd placed at one end of the coffee table, while on the couch and the love seat were five people Buffy didn't know, no doubt fellow MOO members. The comforting scents were coming from the platters of cookies and freshly made snacks amid the pamphlets and what-not on the coffee table, while more of those dreadful dead children signs leaned against every available piece of wall space. She could hear her mom asking someone a question—

"Did you speak to the families on Sycamore Street?"

—before Joyce realized Buffy and Giles were standing in the doorway, obviously agitated.

"Buffy, Mr. Giles." She looked at them, surprised. "Did something happen?"

"Mom, we need to talk to you." She looked at the other people in the room, and they stared back without a trace of friendship or warmth in their expressions. *"Now."*

"Of course, honey." Joyce put the pencil and papers she'd been holding aside and rose. She slipped one hand into the pocket of her sweater. "Go on without me," she said to her guests, then made her way toward Buffy.

"No," Buffy said. "We need to talk *alone*." She turned and let her mother follow her into the entry hall. "There's more going on than you—"

Her mother's hand came around her cheek and clamped over her mouth. Buffy sucked in a lungful of air to protest and realized too late that it was laden with chemicals—chloroform! She wanted to fight, but the effects were instantaneous: tingling shot through her arms and legs, weakening her to the point that she couldn't even push Joyce's hand away. From the corner of her eye she saw Giles's outraged expression turn to disbelief as one of the men from the living room clamped his own chloroform-soaked rag in place over the librarian's mouth and another rushed up and literally lifted Giles's legs out from under him.

As her vision blurred and moved, Buffy's head rolled back to where she could see her mother kneeling by her side and looking down at her. "You were right," she said. Her voice seemed as if it was coming to Buffy's ears through a ten-foot-long cardboard tube. "It was easy."

Buffy wondered who Joyce was talking to, then her head turned even more as she started to fade out, and she saw the two blue-lipped children standing on the stairs and regarding her. Everything about them looked gray and lifeless—even their hair had the same faint dull tone as their skin.

"*I told you,*" the dead little girl said hollowly.

"*It gets even easier,*" the boy added. Balanced on the railing, his left hand was wrapped around the bottle of chloroform.

"*But I'm still scared of the bad girls,*" his sister said.

"*You have to stop them.*" The dead boy—Hans Strauss—regarded Joyce unblinkingly. "*You have to make them go away. Forever.*"

Despite their chilling words, the children's faces remained completely and utterly expressionless, finally whirling down to a tiny dot of pale gray that simply winked away as Buffy passed out.

Chapter 7

Oz and Xander didn't bother to knock, and they found the door to Willow's house closed but not locked.

"Willow!" Oz shouted as they barged through the door. *"Willow!"*

No one answered from downstairs, so both teenagers scrambled up the stairs to the second floor. Their headlong rush into Willow's room stopped dead at what they found inside—

Desk chair overturned, papers everywhere, books that looked as if they'd been thrown across the room. The bedspread and pillows were half on the floor, and Willow's teddy bear lay scrunched in one corner—some of the wall posters had even been knocked askew.

They didn't bother to stick around and ask what happened.

* * *

No, Willow thought. *This isn't happening. This ISN'T happening!*

The rotunda at City Hall, once an attractive if rather stuffy oversized room, had been turned into a stage for execution.

Her execution, and Buffy's, and Amy's.

Willow struggled against the rope that was wound around her and only succeeded in making her mother tighten it even further. To her right, Buffy was similarly bound, upright but unconscious, to a tall, heavy wooden stake driven through a hole in the formerly nicely tiled floor. On the other side of Buffy was Amy, trussed securely in her own winding of rope, and when Willow looked down she saw piles and piles of books—new, old, hardback and paperback. Were those Giles's precious research books at the base of these poles? Was that going to be the fuel for the upcoming pyre?

This isn't happening, Willow thought again, and fought harder.

"Hold still," Sheila said impatiently. "Be a good girl." She tugged on the rope, and Willow felt it tighten painfully around her upper arms.

"No!" Willow cried. "Why are you doing this to me? *Mom?*"

But her mother only shook her head regretfully. "There's no cure but the fire."

"Buffy!" Amy shouted from her spot a couple of yards away. "Wake *up!*"

Willow tried again. "This is *crazy,* Mom!"

"*Buffy!*" Amy wailed.

No good.

The Slayer was still out cold.

* * *

Something vaguely hot stung his cheek, a growing, uncomfortable sensation. Giles groaned and tried to ignore it, but it came again, then again, seemingly harder and more painful each time. After the third time, he forced his eyes open—

"Wake up!"

—just in time to see the hand swoop downward and slap him solidly across the face.

"Cordelia?" he managed.

She took another swing at him, but this time Giles found enough of a reflex to block her. She looked at him petulantly and kneaded her fingers. "Took you long enough to wake up," she said. "My *hand* hurts."

The Watcher rubbed his stinging face. "Pity," he mumbled. Where was he—wait. Buffy's living room. "Why . . . why are you here?"

"Things are *way* out of control, Giles," Cordelia told him as she watched him sit up. "First the thing at school, and then my mom confiscates all of my black clothes and scented candles. I came over here to tell Buffy to stop this craziness, and I found you all unconscious . . . *again*." She regarded him curiously. "How many times have you been knocked out, anyway? I swear, one of these times you're going to wake up in a coma."

Giles scrunched his eyes shut briefly. "Wake up in—oh, never mind. We need to save Buffy from Hansel and Gretel."

Cordelia stared at him for a second, then pressed her lips together and took his elbow to help him to his feet. "Now let's be clear: the brain damage happened *before* I hit you, right?"

Oz and Xander had headed for City Hall at a dead run, but the race screeched to an abrupt end in the hallway outside the entrance to the rotunda.

Four husky men, the infamous MOO buttons pinned proudly to their shirts, blocked their way. To add insult to everything about the situation, the rear two paused just long enough to shoot the two teenagers a dirty look before turning back and locking the door.

"What's with the grim?" Xander punned in a falsely cheerful voice. "We're here to join you guys."

None of the men answered. They just pressed forward, faces like unforgiving stone statues, muscles bulging in folded arms.

"No, really," Xander said brightly. "Why should *you* guys have all the fun? We want to be part of the hate."

No effect—if anything, the expressions of the collective mob only became more murderous. Oz raised an eyebrow. "Just so we're clear," he said with absolutely no sarcasm, "you guys know you're nuts, right?"

And he and Xander hightailed it in the opposite direction, with the MOO goons grunting and running right behind them.

Panic was fast running through Willow's nerves. The situation was bad enough, but Buffy was still unconscious—what had they done to her? Did she have a concussion, or even something worse? She tried again, raising her voice in an effort to be heard over the muttering, shifting crowd in front of the three poles. *"Buffy!"*

No response—no, wait. Yes, her friend was finally coming to! Buffy's head came up, then fell forward again, then came up a second time with a jerk as her surroundings sank in and she opened her eyes wide. Willow could see her friend trying to comprehend everything through the leftover grogginess of whatever she'd been dosed with.

Mrs. Summers was there and waiting, standing right

below where she had bound her daughter to the stake in the ground. "Good morning, sleepyhead." Considering what was going on, Willow thought it was the most ludicrous thing she'd ever heard.

"Mom," Buffy said. "You don't want this." Her voice was growing stronger with every word.

But Buffy's mom only gazed up at her sorrowfully. "Since when does it matter what I want?" she asked. "I wanted a normal, happy daughter. Instead I got a Slayer."

Buffy stared at her, shocked, then glanced over at Willow with a stricken expression. Before Willow could say anything, her mother walked up to Mrs. Summers and offered her something.

"Torch?" she said pleasantly.

"Thanks," Buffy's mother said, and took it. Willow could only watch, speechless, as the two women chatted as if they were doing nothing more important than discussing the schedule of the next neighborhood council meeting. Joyce sighed. "This has been so trying, but you've been such a champ."

Willow's mother nodded agreeably. "Oh, you, too, Joyce."

Mrs. Summers perked up a bit. "We should stay close," she suggested. "Have lunch."

"Oh, I'd like that," Sheila said. "How nice."

Her mother's voice was placid and unemotional, and it made Willow just want to scream—was her mother in a trance or what? Didn't she realize what was going on here? For crying out loud, she had *fire* in her hands, and in another minute she'd be having the barbecued daughter special!

"Oh, you can't be serious!" Amy said as the two mothers leaned over and used their torches to light fires in the books surrounding the base of each stake.

"Mom, *don't!*" Buffy yelled.

Too late—flames were already spreading among the pages and sending small, bright towers of heated yellow to dance only a few feet away from each girl. Willow's own terror was bad enough, but the sight of the fire so close to her feet sent Amy into absolute ballistics.

"All right!" she shouted furiously at the crowd. She tried to twist within the ropes but succeeded only in vibrating the stake that held her. "You want to fry a witch? I'll *give* you a witch!" Willow's eyes widened as Amy threw back her head and started to chant, gazing up toward the stars. *"Goddess Hecate, work thy will—"*

Willow's gaze met Buffy's, and Willow futilely tried to think—had she heard these words before?

Her best friend looked back toward Amy, and even within her bindings, Buffy cringed. "Uh-oh."

Willow craned her neck until she could just see Amy, then wished she hadn't. Her once pretty eyes had gone completely coal black, and her body was shaking as her improvised spell began to work its magic.

"—before thee let the unclean thing crawl!"

A sound split the air, like muffled thunder, and Amy's body was suddenly encircled with a line of glowing white light dancing with sparkling purple spots. The MOO crowd gave a collective gasp and fell back, some covering their eyes as the light grew to blinding proportions and peaked. And when it was gone in a final puff of white and pink-tinted smoke—

—so was Amy.

Or not, Willow thought as she glimpsed a dark form—a small, sleek rat—dart from the pile of Amy's clothes that had billowed into an empty mass at the base of her stake.

The fleeing rodent was not lost on Buffy. "She couldn't do us first?" she demanded as the rat disappeared between the feet in the crowd.

So much for Amy's show-stopping abilities—the crowd was already slinking back into place, hungry to get their front-row seats for the big roasting.

Willow inhaled, searching for courage. "You've seen what we can do!" she shouted at the crowd, trying to make herself as loud as she could. "Another step and you will *all* feel my power!"

"What are you going to do?" Buffy whispered at her. "Float a pencil at them?"

Despite Buffy's doubt, there did seem to her to be a sudden sense of hesitation in the attitude of the people crowding around. She made her voice even more fierce and frightening, so loud her throat actually hurt. "It's a really *big* power!"

Buffy must have noticed the way the MOO people were falling back, too, because she decided to join in on Willow's threats. The more, the merrier. "Yes! You will all be turned into vermin—and some of you will be *fish!* Yeah, you in the back will be fish—"

Willow could have sunk to her knees with relief—well, if it hadn't been for the annoying rope around her—when she saw that their words were definitely having an effect. People were backing away from the would-be pyres, and even her mom and Mrs. Summers suddenly seemed less than sure about their actions.

"Maybe we should go," someone in the crowd said, and Willow heard murmurs of agreement.

"But you promised . . ."

The high, sweet voice of a child cut over everything, making the crowd fall silent in a way that even Amy's incantation of a few moments ago had failed to accomplish. So shocked was she by what she saw that for a moment Willow forgot where she was and what was happening. Was that really the "dead" little boy of the MOO posters, standing right in front of the crowd and speaking to her mother and Mrs. Summers? And with him was the girl—

"You have to kill the bad girls,"

—her own sickly, toneless voice adding to his words and rolling over the paralyzed people like a proclamation of broken vows and guilt.

CHAPTER 8

"I can't believe you had this stuff in your apartment,"
Cordelia said in disgust. "It smells foul."

Giles ignored her tone and tried to coax a little more
speed out of the old car, at the same time trying to pry Old
World German out of his brain's memory banks. "Shred
the wolfsbane—that's the leafy stuff," he instructed her.
"Then you can crush the satyrion root." He slowed and
turned left, then pressed on the accelerator again. *"Luften
sie den . . .* something. *Schumer? Schluter?"*

"God," Cordelia grumbled. "This is *killing* my mani-
cure." She frowned at him. "What are you muttering
about?"

"It's part of an incantation," he told her. "It's in German, but without my books . . ."

"What does it mean?"

"It's about lifting a veil," he answered. "It should make
the demons appear in their true form, which with any luck

74

should negate their influence." Giles glanced quickly at what she was doing. "Oh—and you need to drop a toad-stone into the mixture."

Cordelia poked around in the small bag of things he'd quickly put together back at his place. "This?" She sniffed it curiously. "It doesn't look like a toad."

Almost there—just another block or so. "No reason it should," he said absently. "It's from inside the toad."

For a moment the teenage girl said nothing, then she grimaced. "I *hate* you."

Oz wasn't quite sure how they'd managed it, but somehow he and Xander had ended up in an unfamiliar part of City Hall—too many zigzagged turns and twists, stairwells and switchbacks in trying to throw off the MOO goons. They'd succeeded, but the two of them were pretty well lost, not sure now which way was in or out, and they certainly had no idea where Willow and Amy were. Worse, they'd gotten themselves into some kind of closed-off area, and while the thugs chasing them hadn't yet picked up the trail, they couldn't be that far behind.

Frustrated, he and Xander tried the last set of doors that might offer a way out, but when they slammed their shoulders into it—

Locked, of course.

Oz started to say something, then he and Xander both jerked as a faint but familiar voice wafted from overhead.

"No! Oh, God—help!"

Oz's eyes widened. "Will?"

"It sounds like she's right . . . above us?" Xander pointed at an oversized air vent up near the ceiling. They glanced at each other, then Oz scrambled on top of the file cabinet beneath it. Another second, and he'd knocked in the aluminum cover and crawled into the ventilation system with Xander close behind.

Willow saw that the flames were spreading, and it seemed their destruction was inescapable.

The dead little children were still there, pressing closer. The golden firelight dancing on their skin did nothing to dispel its gray pallor, added no warmth to their eyes or expressions. Their voices were high and clear, dull with accusation.

"They hurt us," the little girl said plaintively.

"Burn them," added her brother.

Beside her, Buffy struggled uselessly against the heavy rope and tried to get through to her mother. "Mom, *dead people are talking to you*—do that math!"

But Mrs. Summers just stood there as though she were hypnotized, watching the fire move closer. "I'm sorry, Buffy."

"Mom, *look* at me!" Buffy shouted. "You *love* me. You're not going to be able to live with yourself if you do this!"

Buffy's mother only shook her head. "You *earned* this," she pointed out quietly. "You toyed with unnatural forces. What kind of a mother would I be if I didn't punish you?"

Although he and Cordelia had finally made it to City Hall, Giles soon discovered that his troubles weren't over just yet.

There were no guards, but Giles wasn't convinced that was a good thing—it was far too likely that they were off tormenting someone else or inside the locked rotunda area and cheering on whatever terrible escapades were taking place. He could hear shouting from the other side, but the doors were heavy, and he couldn't make out the words or even whether the voices were male or female. They *had* to get in there.

He spun indecisively, then focused on Cordelia waiting impatiently a few feet away, the small vial of completed potion clutched in one delicate hand. Without asking, he reached out and snatched a pin from the mass of dark brown curls piled atop her head.

"Ow!" She glared at him. "You got hair with that!"

The librarian ignored her and knelt so that he was eye level with the lock. He shoved the pin in and began working it carefully back and forth.

"God," Cordelia said in contempt. "You really were the little youthful offender, weren't you? You must just look back on that and cringe."

Giles shot her an aggravated look. "Shhhh!" If he could just get this last, tricky part to turn . . .

The heat washed over her, and over her, and over her again, until Willow felt like a steak in a frying pan. Yellow sparkles teased at the edges of her vision, warning signs of impending unconsciousness. "Buffy," she tried, and barely managed to turn her head toward her friend. "I—I can't take it—it's too hot!"

Buffy looked more miserable than in pain. "I'm sorry, Will—if it wasn't for me, none of this would have happened. It wouldn't be—" She broke off suddenly, and Willow forced herself to gaze where Buffy was looking. There, far in the back, she saw the main doors to the rotunda ease open as Giles and Cordelia slipped inside.

Another wave of hot air blasted her in the face, and Willow looked down and saw a book directly below her feet burst into flames.

Yes, Giles and Cordelia had come to help . . .
But were they in time?

Giles was nearly stunned into immobility by the sight that greeted him and Cordelia when he got the rotunda doors opened and they slipped through.

If it hadn't been for the lights of City Hall shining through the frosted glass windows and into the rotunda, he would have thought they'd stumbled across an old-fashioned witch burning in England. There were three stakes, and trussed to two of them like chickens waiting to be roasted were Buffy and Willow—it was likely that the third had once held Amy, although he couldn't fathom how the girl had escaped. Books—his, no doubt, plus others confiscated around the town by MOO's disciples—littered the ground beneath each stake, the fodder for the fires that were burning perilously close to the feet of the two girls. Incredibly, both Joyce Summers and Sheila Rosenberg simply stood there, apparently mesmerized by the vision of their children going up in flames.

Giles scanned the room and spotted a firebox off to the side. He pointed Cordelia in that direction, assuming she'd simply open the door and take out the hose. Wrong, of course—for some reason known only to a teenager's mind, the girl opted instead for the much louder access route of smashing the glass in the door.

The crash of the glass broke the trancelike hold over the two women and their MOO associates, but Giles had no choice but to leave Cordelia in charge of the rescue aspects—heaven help them—and start the incantation. Drat it, he knew the words in English, but his German had never been good enough to enable him to do that all-important thing required for true fluency in a second language—he couldn't actually *think* in German. To speak it, especially on something about which he wasn't sure, he still found it necessary to run the words through his mind first.

Demons, show yourselves, the Watcher thought. *I call on the powers of Hecate, queen and protectress of witches, to strip away the masks. Let evil wear an evil face—*

"*Uh, Dämonen zeigen sich,*" Giles announced, hoping desperately that he was getting the order of the words correct. "*Ich um die Energien von Hecate heraufbeschwören, Königin und Schützer von der Hexen, zu Streifen weg die Masken. Lassen Sie Übel ein übles Gesicht anzeihen.*"

"Stop them!" Joyce Summers cried.

A dozen people and more whirled to face them, but Cordelia yanked out the fire hose and managed to twist the valve at the end; when they tried to rush her and Giles, she used the force of the water to keep them at bay. She fought with the hose and sent would-be attackers slipping and stumbling backward as Giles continued trying to recite his unveiling spell.

"Buffy!" he heard Willow wail. "I'm on fire!"

"Cordelia, *put out the fire!*" Buffy shouted over the voices of the crowd. For a tortuous moment, Cordelia actually looked surprised, then she focused the blast of the water hose toward the flames licking at the feet of Willow and Buffy.

As the fires around the rotunda sputtered and went out and Cordelia twisted the hose shut, the crowd and the smoke suddenly parted. For a moment Giles's words faltered as he saw the two children—the *dead* ones—step from the gathering of people and walk toward him, their expressions condemning. He tried to think faster, to *translate* faster—*Hecate implores you, lift the veil, lift the veil, hide not behind false faces*—then finally just blurted out the rest the best he could. *"Hecate Sie inständig bitten. Heben Sie den Schleier an. Heben Sie den Schleier an. Verstecken Sie sich nicht hinter falschen Gesichtern!"*

With the final words of the incantation, Giles threw the glass vial at the feet of the kids.

It broke, splashing their ankles with the steaming potion. Mist boiled upward from the liquid, and the children recoiled, then turned toward each other and embraced. An instant later the tiny forms were melding together and elongating, growing upward and lengthening until the figure that stood before the terrified crowd was not at all that of either of the innocent-faced murder victims who had stood there only a second before.

What faced them now was big, hairy, and incredibly frightening.

"Okay," Cordelia said weakly. "I think I liked the two little ones more than the one big one."

The ghastly-looking demon was at least seven feet tall, with pointed ears, wiry hair that stuck out everywhere, and sores and warts all over a mostly unclothed form. Its eyes glowed red above an elongated nose and a mouthful of sharp teeth that included two tusklike protrusions from its bottom jaw. Bony chest heaving, it swung to face the crowd, its leathery face creased with fury. *"Protect us! Kill the bad girls!"* it commanded in a loud, sandpaper voice.

Instead of obeying, the people in the crowd screamed and scattered. Only Joyce and Sheila remained, frozen and incredulous.

"You know what?" Buffy called sarcastically. "Not as convincing in that outfit."

Giles watched helplessly as the demon, enraged at its failure, turned toward Buffy and charged.

Buffy jerked, then wrenched her body sideways and finally succeeded in breaking off the heavy, pointed stake to which she was tied. She bent over and braced herself just as the demon surged forward with a snarl, and Giles saw her body shudder with the impact of his leap.

Then everything just . . . stopped as Giles and the crowd realized that the Slayer had embedded her makeshift weapon directly into the base of the hellish demon's throat.

Facing the ground and stuck, unable to straighten up but not knowing why, all Buffy could do was turn her head sideways as she tried to see. "Did I get it? Did I get it?"

Giles started to step forward, then the ceiling directly in front of where the three stakes had been set up collapsed. Two figures plummeted to the floor along with the pieces of a broken air-conditioning vent and landed amid the sodden remains of the partially burned books—

Oz and Xander.

With Xander stunned at his side, Oz twisted around in the mess until he could look up at Willow. "We're here to save you," he said.

EPILOGUE

Willow sat cross-legged on the floor in front of the bed with Buffy across from her, carefully arranging the ingredients for the upcoming spell. All the usual stuff was there—candles, herbs and dried roots, a little spell bowl to burn the stuff in. They were just about ready.

Buffy eyed the layout critically. "Your mom doesn't mind us doing this in the house?"

Willow gave her friend a little smile. "She doesn't know."

"Ah." Buffy glanced at her sympathetically. "Business as usual?"

"Sort of." Willow shrugged and added a final pinch of a special herb conglomeration to the bowl. "She's doing that selective memory thing your mom used to be so good at."

Buffy's eyebrows raised. "She forgot *everything?*"

Now Willow grinned outright. "No. She remembered the part where I said I was dating a musician. Oz has to come for dinner next week." She peered at Buffy. "So that's sort of like taking an interest."

Her best friend nodded, then sat back. "Okay—shall we try this again?"

"Let do it," Willow said firmly. "I think we got the mix of herbs right this time."

Buffy leaned forward and dropped a little clump of brown hair into the spell bowl, then lit the whole concoction with a match. A thick plume of pink smoke rose, swirling in the air between the two girls.

"Diana, Hecate—I hereby license thee to depart," Willow intoned. "Goddess of creatures, great and small, I conjure thee to withdraw!"

As the smoke finally cleared, Willow and Buffy looked to the side hopefully.

And there, still, waited the Amyrat, sitting up as it watched them with quivering whiskers and tiny eyes full of expectation.

Buffy looked at Willow, then again at the rat, and Willow could only shrug.

"Maybe we should get her one of those wheel thingies," Buffy said.

DAILY JOURNAL ENTRY:

See, I haven't been bad at all about
keeping my computer journal up to date.
It's only been a little while since my
last entry, but even so, there's so much
to record. Sometimes I just can't believe everything that's happened, some
really *huge* stuff.

Likes Giles getting *fired*.

No, not from the library—he's still
there, of course. I mean, if you checked
him out medical-wise, I'm sure we'd find
out that books (especially the really *old*
ones) are like part of his DNA chain or
something. He got canned by the Watchers Council, of all things—can you imagine? Some bunch of old . . . well, older . . .
English fuddy-duddies sitting around a
table somewhere across the Atlantic,
drinking their tea and making decisions
like this when they're not even here to
see on a day-to-day basis what Giles
does? Plus, it was for a totally bogus
reason!

See, apparently they have this test,
called a Cruiciamentum, that they give
to Slayers on their eighteenth birth-
days—like Slayers don't have a seriously
compromised life span *anyway*. So Giles
got ordered to give Buffy this stuff
that kind of . . . I don't know . . . sucked

all her Slayer strength away. Then they tell Giles he has to lock her up with this psycho-vampire and see if she survives. Well, *duh*.

Needless to say, Giles caved and told her about the whole thing—he couldn't bear to take the chance she would get hurt, and so they fired him, said he *cared* too much for her. Some reason, huh?

So now we've got Wesley Wyndam-Pryce, another British guy who's younger than Giles but, well, not the biggest splinter off the stake, if you get my meaning. Strangely enough, Cordelia of all people seems attracted to him, but Buffy won't listen to him, and Faith didn't want anything to do with him—

Oh, yeah . . . Faith. Mondo-sized problem there. Faith is a whole 'nother bad. For a while she and Buffy were really tight, and to tell you the truth I was starting to feel a little left out. Then Faith made a mistake and killed Allan Finch, the deputy mayor—a *human* man—and didn't even regret it when she realized her mistake. To cap it, she tried to blame it on Buffy, though Giles saw through her lie. Right now there's kind of an uneasy truce between Faith and Buffy, and who knows what'll happen with that.

Meanwhile, from what I can tell, Cordelia has a new flunky, some girl named Anya who's as well dressed as she is. I guess she transferred here or something—which is a little weird, it being the middle of the school year—but it's probably nice for Cordelia to have someone new around. Especially since her friends have basically shunned her since learning that a "loser" like Xander cheated on her.

No luck, yet, in changing Amy back to a human. Her spell seemed so simple—*"before thee let the unclean thing crawl"*—but I can't even reverse it. I feel bad for thinking it, kind of guilty because Amy was my friend, but . . . why would she say something like that, use a spell so dark-sided? Was it an instinctive reflection of her inner self, a part of her that I never knew about? Is that why she turned into a rat, instead of, say, a cat or a cute little bunny? I mean, why didn't she say "before thee let the soft white thing run" or "the fast feline flee"? Heck, *anything* would've been better than being turned into a rat. Well, except maybe a snake or something like that.

The point is, what happened to Amy, what she ultimately turned out to be . . . well, that really makes me wonder what's inside a person sometimes, and what's inside the people we think we know best—or inside all of us.

Even what's inside me . . .

/PRESS ENTER TO SAVE FILE/

FILE: DOPPELGÄNGLAND

PROLOGUE

Candles flickered around a dim room in which the air was thick with scented incense. The demon D'Hoffryn, looking magnificently evil, sat cross-legged upon a stone altar and stared downward at the woman who had summoned him, his pale, wrinkled face appropriately displeased. His eyes glittered, and the triple horns on either side of his head bobbed above his pointed ears as he sneered out his words.

"Do not ask again!"

Anya knelt on the cold floor and felt her stomach clench more in frustration than fury. "B-but—"

"Your powers were a gift of the lower beings. You have proved unworthy of them."

"I was robbed of them!"

"By your carelessness," D'Hoffryn hissed.

Anya drew herself up proudly. "For a thousand years I wielded the powers of the wish. I brought ruin upon the heads of unfaithful men, I brought forth destruction and chaos for the pleasure of the lower beings—I was feared and worshiped across the mortal globe—and now I'm *stuck* at Sunnydale High!" Her mouth twisted. "A *mortal*—a child!" She looked even more distressed. "And I'm flunking math."

D'Hoffryn waved a clawed hand at her, and the three prongs of his beard jiggled. "That is no concern of ours. You will live out your mortal life and die."

"Give me another chance," Anya pleaded, leaning forward. "You can fold the fabric of time—send me back to that place, and I'll change it. I won't fail again."

The demon's head lifted, and he glared down at her. "Your time is passed," he said.

Anya felt desperation sweep over her. "Do you have any idea how boring twelfth-graders are?" When he just looked at her, completely disinterested, she drew herself to her feet. "I'm *getting* my power center back," she said angrily. "And if you won't help me, then by the pestilent gods, I'll find someone who will!"

She didn't look back as she stormed out of the room.

CHAPTER 1

Days like this, Willow thought, *could make a body think Sunnydale was as normal as anywhere else in the country.*

Lunch break outside, and she lay on her belly on the grass and propped herself up on her elbows, ankles crossed and swaying idly in the air. Beautiful weather—not too chilly, not too hot—and her long-sleeved shirt was just right. There was a light breeze, and it was slightly overcast but not depressing, perfect because she didn't have to squint against the sun as she focused her entire attention on the pencil a few inches in front of her fingers.

Focus . . .

Focus . . .

Yes.

It rose, staying perfectly horizontal because she wanted it that way. When it got to nose level she concentrated a bit harder, and after a moment it began to spin gently, like a child's pinwheel drawn through the air.

BUFFY THE VAMPIRE SLAYER

"The Watchers Council shrink is heavily into tests," Buffy said from a few feet away. Her friend was lying on her back under one of the big shade trees and doing stomach crunches. Willow had stopped counting them a while ago. "He's got tests for everything—TATs, Rorschach, associative logic." Finally she stopped and sat up. "They have that test to see if you're crazy, the one that asks if you ever hear voices or if you've ever wanted to be a florist."

"Oh!" Willow said, turning her head toward Buffy. "I used to—wait. Florist means crazy, right?" She shook her head emphatically. "I never wanted to do that."

Buffy's gaze cut past her to the pencil still spinning lazily in the air. "Neat."

"Thanks," Willow said with a grin. "It's all about emotional control. Plus, obviously, magic." She perked up. "Hey, you want to go to the Espresso Pump and get sugared up on mochas?"

"Pass," Buffy answered. She started stuffing her things into her gym bag. "I'm going to hit the pool and do some laps."

Willow peered at her. "How come the sudden calisthenics? Aren't you sort of naturally buff, Buff?" She giggled, pleased at her little funny. "Buff Buff!"

But Buffy's return smile was less than enthusiastic. "Well, they've really got us running around on the physical side, too. A lot of reflex evaluation and precision training. You know. I just want to . . . do . . ."

"Better than Faith?" Willow finished for her.

Buffy looked ashamed. "So very shallow."

Willow sat up. "Competition is natural and healthy," she told her friend. "Plus you'll definitely ace her on the psych tests. Just don't mark the box that says 'I sometimes like to kill people.'"

Buffy smiled a little sadly. "I know Faith's not going to

94

be on the cover of *Sanity Fair,* but she's had it rough. Given different circumstances, that could be me."

"No way," Willow said flatly.

Buffy looked at the ground. "We can't control the way we grow up."

"No," Willow disagreed. "You're you. She's her. Some people just don't have that in them."

Buffy ran a hand through her hair, then pulled her gym bag toward her. "Look, I'm sorry—I know you hate talking about Faith."

"No, it's okay," Willow assured her.

"No, really," Buffy insisted. "We should just—"

"No, it doesn't bother me." Willow made her voice firm. "I mean it."

For a moment her friend said nothing. Then, "Uh . . . Will?"

Willow followed the direction of Buffy's gaze and saw the pencil, still in the air but no longer gently spinning. Instead it looked like the Number Two version of a lawnmower blade, revolving so fast all she could make out was a circular blur.

"Oooh," she said in a small voice. Willow tried to channel her thoughts enough to stop the pencil's motion and succeeded only in sending it cutting across the air between them as it embedded itself point first into the trunk of the tree.

"Emotional control?" Buffy asked, sounding faintly amused.

Willow winced. "I'm . . . working on it."

Principal Snyder's office.

Or Sunnydale Cemetery at, say, two A.M.

Willow was having a hard time deciding which would be the worse choice, although right now, as she sat on a chair facing Principal Snyder's desk, Sunnydale Cemetery was right up there with Hawaii in January. The chair next to her held a slouching example of one of Sunnydale High's premium basketball jocks, Percy West.

"As far as I'm concerned, this is a marriage made in heaven," Principal Snyder said to both of them as he hung his coat on the coat tree in the corner. "Willow Rosenberg, despite her . . . unsavory associations, represents the pinnacle of academic achievement at Sunnydale High. Percy West represents a devastating fast break and fifty percent from behind the three-point line." The ratty little man gave Percy a companionable slap on the shoulder as he walked around to his chair.

Willow swallowed and twisted her fingers together. "I'm . . . not sure I understand the marriage part."

The principal regarded her blandly. "You've got the brains, he's got the fast break. It's a perfect match."

"Match?" She glanced nervously at Percy, who only scratched at something on his temple. "You want us to . . . breed?"

Snyder ignored her. "I want you to tutor him. Percy is flunking history." The older man sat and folded his hands. "Nothing seems to be able to motivate him."

"Hey," Percy said, finally deciding to add something to the conversation. "I'm challenged."

Snyder was unconvinced. "You're lazy, self-involved, and spoiled. That's quite the challenge." Instead of answering, Percy wiped his mouth on one sleeve. "But we need a winning year," Snyder continued, "especially after last year's debacle with the swim team. Can't have our point guard benched." He turned his beady gaze on Willow. "So you are going to take on a little teaching job. I know how you enjoy teaching."

"But I have a lot of work of my own—" Willow began.

"You've gotten a letter of acceptance from every university with a stamp," Snyder interrupted. "I think your academic career is safe."

Percy found something interesting on the ceiling to stare at while Willow fidgeted. "Yes, but I still have classes, and I don't want—"

"Rosenberg, it's time to give something *back* to the community," Snyder said in a disgustingly sweet tone. He stood, and for such a little smidgen of a man, Willow suddenly felt he was very big, as if he was *looming* over her, in fact. "I know you want to help your school out here. Ask me how I know."

She knew it was useless, but she had to anyway. "How do y—"

Principal Snyder stared hard at her. "I just *do.*"

It was just so totally unfair that Percy West could sit there and look completely and utterly bored, while she felt as if Snyder had just threatened to put her in detention for a month if she didn't do what he wanted.

"So he threatened you?" Buffy asked incredulously. "With *what?*"

"It wasn't anything exactly that he said," Willow explained as she and Buffy came into the library. "It was all in his eyes. I mean, there was some nostril work as well . . . but mostly eyes."

What a pal—Buffy sounded totally peeved on her behalf. "Snyder needs me to kick his butt."

"Oh, no, Buffy—don't get in trouble." Willow dumped her books on the library table. "I just hate the way he bullies people. He just assumes their time is *his.*"

"Willow," Giles said from behind them. She turned and saw him step out of his office, cherry-flavored sucker in one hand. "Get on the computer. I want you to take another pass at accessing the Mayor's files."

"Okay," she said, and slipped off her bag before going behind the counter and settling in front of the computer. A good spot, because she could work on the computer stuff but still be a part of what was going on, so she heard Faith breeze into the library with Wesley lurching along behind her.

"Well," Faith said cheerfully. "That was a blast."

Giles regarded her, then looked at Wesley. "How did it go?"

"Princess Margaret here had a little trouble keeping up," Faith said with a sneer. When Willow glanced at her, Faith looked absurdly fresh, not at all like someone who'd just been put through a bunch of physical paces.

"How did it *go?*" Giles asked again. He stared pointedly at Wesley.

"Faith . . . did quite well on the obstacle field," Wesley finally said between gasps. "And her . . . reflexes are improving rapidly." He sucked in air, then, despite his discomfort, managed to look down his nose at the dark-haired Slayer. *"Physically* she's in good shape. Still a little sloppy, though."

Willow saw Faith glare at Wesley, but before she could say anything, Giles asked, "Do you feel up to taking Buffy out, or shall I?"

"No, no," Wesley said between inhalations. "I'll be fine. Just give me a minute . . . and some defibrillators, if it's not too much trouble."

Faith grinned at Buffy. "You're gonna love it, B. It's just like fun . . . only boring."

"Faith," Giles said sternly, "this evaluation is a necessary part of—"

"I know," she cut in, sounding contrite. "I'm on board here. Just . . . shooting my mouth off."

"I'd better change," Buffy said, and headed for the locker room while Giles and Wesley retreated into the librarian's office.

As Buffy passed Faith, Willow thought she was seeing things when the rival Slayer reached out and touched Buffy's shoulder. "Good luck."

Buffy smiled in response and kept going, then Faith turned and wandered over to the counter. After a second, she hopped up onto it and sat, peering over to where Willow worked steadily on the computer's keyboard. "Whatcha doing?"

"I'm trying to access the Mayor's personal files," Willow answered with forced politeness. Darn it, no matter what she'd told Buffy earlier, she just wasn't comfortable around Faith.

Faith blinked, surprised at Willow's words. "Can you do that?"

Willow shrugged, still feeling self-conscious around the other girl. "He's got some pretty tricky barriers set up."

Faith was silent for a moment. "Can you get past them?"

"Eventually I'll get through," Willow replied.

Faith didn't say anything else, so Willow kept working, trying to concentrate and wondering vaguely about Faith's sudden, strange interest in the computer aspect of Slayage.

CHAPTER 2

"**W**ell," Mayor Wilkins said thoughtfully as he digested the information she'd just given him. "That's very interesting."

Faith nodded. "Yeah, I thought so, too." She tried but just couldn't keep her mind focused on Willow's little underhanded attempts at cruising the Mayor's computer realm. Instead, she backed up and spun, trying to take in everything at once about the apartment the Mayor had announced only moments before was . . . *hers*. "Are you serious about this place?"

"Of course I am," he said emphatically. "No Slayer of mine is going to live in a fleabag hotel. That place has a very unsavory reputation. There are immoral liaisons going on there."

"Plus all the screwing," Faith agreed. "This is the kick!" She strode around the oversized, great-room setup, noting the big stuffed chaise longue and chair in the living room area, the tiny dining set by the big curved window, lamps everywhere—there was even a heavy bag strung from a chain in the ceiling so she could work out. *Awesome!*

"We'll keep your old place," the Mayor told her. He seemed to get a charge out of her delight in her new place to crash. "In case you need to see your friends there. But from now on—"

Faith spotted the bed—a queen-sized thing behind gauzy blue curtains—and ran to it, leaped up, and starting jumping up and down on it excitedly. *Just like a kid in a candy store,* she thought giddily, *given everything I always wanted and thought I'd never have!*

"Oh, hey—hey!" Mayor Wilkins said sharply. "Shoes—shoes!"

She hopped down obediently, bouncing to a stop directly in front of him. With an inviting smile, she stepped up close and placed her hands on either side of his lapels. "Thanks, Sugar Daddy."

But he only frowned at her. "Now, Faith, I don't find that sort of thing amusing. I'm a family man." He stepped away, and so did she, relieved. That feeling, however, turned to hesitation at his next words. "Now," he said calmly, "let's kill your little friend." He held up a hand when he saw her expression. "Don't worry—I wouldn't ask you to do it, not this early in our relationship. Besides, I think a vampire attack would look less suspicious, anyway."

Faith nodded, still not sure of what to say. Kill Willow? Was she really up to something like that?

"In the meantime," Mayor Wilkins said with a smile, "let's take a look at the rest of the apartment, huh? If I'm not mistaken, some lucky girl has herself a PlayStation."

Her eyes widened. She'd always wanted one. "No way!"

But the Mayor just grinned at her and nodded—
"Yes, way."
—as he led her toward the other room.

"Hey," Oz said.

Willow smiled as her boyfriend stopped her in the hallway between classes. "Oz . . . hi."

"There's something about you that's causing me to hug you," he said as he slipped his arms around her and squeezed lightly. "It's like I have no will of my own."

She couldn't help grinning as they started in the direction of their next classes. "Where were you yesterday?" she asked.

"We got back late," he said casually. "Sort of very."

Willow had no idea what he was talking about. "We? Who? Where?"

"The band," he answered. "We had a gig in Monterey on Sunday night."

"Oh . . . you did?" Jeez, could she be any more out of the loop when she didn't even know her boyfriend's band was playing somewhere? "How come I didn't know?" She had to ask.

But Oz just looked at her, not understanding. "I thought you did."

"Maybe I would have liked to go," Willow said. She hugged her schoolbooks, not trying to hide her hurt.

Oz raised an eyebrow. "Didn't figure you for missing school," he said. Then he added, "Never thought to ask."

A terrible thought struck her. "You think I'm boring."

"I'd call that a radical interpretation of the text." He looked at her somewhat quizzically. When she didn't answer, he touched her arm. "We're playing tonight at the Bronze."

Willow's expression fell. "I . . . can't. I have too much homework."

Oz nodded. "If you get done early . . ." he suggested, and left it at that as he headed off.

She watched him go, then cut across the Quad toward her own class, thinking that maybe she'd make a quick stop at her locker, when she saw Percy West up ahead. She hurried to catch up.

"Percy—hey," she said when he finally realized she was there and decided to slow down a bit. "Listen, I thought we could get together today at lunch and go over your Roosevelt paper, what books you'll need and stuff—"

He gave her a disbelieving glance, then picked up his pace again. "What are you talking about?"

"Tutoring you," Willow reminded him. "Your history paper?"

"Oh, yeah," Percy said carelessly. "Snyder said you were gonna do it."

She would have stopped cold, but then he would have just kept going. "He never said that."

"What meeting were *you* at?" he asked with a smirk.

"Look," Willow said, trying to be firm. "I'll get the books you need. Just meet me at lunch, and we'll—"

"I don't have time at lunch," the jock interrupted. "Gotta hang out."

"Oh. Well—"

He finally stopped and faced her. "What?" he demanded rudely. "You got something better to do? Just type it up and put my name on it." He started to waltz off, then paused one last time. "And don't type too good—dead giveaway."

She stood there as he left, speechless, then stomped over to a bench and dropped onto it. Well, today was going just great, wasn't it, what with Snyder and Percy, and then of course the whole thing with Oz and not even knowing he'd been out of town last night. Cranky, Willow shook off her backpack, then rummaged around in it until she found her lunch bag. Feeling rebellious, she dug into it and pulled out the banana. "I'm going to eat this *now*," she said in a low voice. "It's not lunchtime, I don't even care."

"Hey."

Before she could peel it, Willow raised her head and saw Buffy standing there with Xander. Both of them seemed obscenely happy in contrast to the way she felt.

Xander leaned toward her. "Willow, did you remember to tape *Biography* last Friday?"

She clenched her teeth. "Uh-huh."

"See," Buffy said smugly to Xander. "I told you—Old Reliable."

Willow's fingers tightened around the banana, bruising it. "Oh, *thanks*," she said bitterly.

"What?" Buffy asked, taken aback.

"Old Reliable," Willow grumbled. "Yeah, great—there's a sexy nickname."

Buffy immediately looked apologetic. "Oh, Will, I didn't mean it as—"

"No, it's fine." She stared at her half-crushed banana. "I'm Old Reliable."

Xander gave her a goofy smile. "She just meant, you know, the geyser—you're like a geyser of fun that goes off at regular intervals."

"That's Old Faithful," Willow said.

Xander looked puzzled. "Isn't that the dog that the guy has to shoot—"

Willow grimaced. "That's Old *Yeller*."

"Xander," Buffy cut in. "I *beg* you not to help me." She

Willow Rosenberg

Wicca Will

"Another step and you will all see my
power.... It's a really big power."
—Willow

Hans and Greta Straus

"I was supposed to lead us in a moment of silence, but silence is this town's disease."

—Joyce Summers

Reliable dog geyser person vamps it up.

BUFFY: "Just remember, a vampire's personality has nothing to do with the person it was."

ANGEL: "Well, actually — (off Buffy's glare) — that's a good point."

"Bored now."
— Vamp Willow

"So Faith is like 'I'm
gonna beat you up,'
and I'm all 'I'm not
afraid of you,' and
then she had the knife
and that was less fun
but oh! I told her,
'You made your
choice, Buffy was
your friend . . . .'"

—Willow

Gavrok spiders

"You ... all of you. ... Why couldn't you be normal?"
—Principal Snyder

turned to Willow. "Will, I didn't mean it in a bad way. I think it's good to be reliable."

Enough already. Willow grabbed her backpack and stuffed the lunch bag haphazardly into it. "Well, maybe I don't *want* to be reliable all the time," she snapped. "Maybe I'm not just some doormat . . . *person.* Homework Gal."

Xander gulped. "I'm thinking nerve strike."

She stood and jerked on her pack, then stopped, even angrier, for one last comment before leaving. "Maybe I'll change my look," she said hotly. "You don't know." She brandished the banana. "And I'm *eating* this banana—lunchtime be damned!"

She took off but hadn't taken three steps before she realized Buffy was following her. "Wait," her friend said. "I'm really sorry. I—"

Willow stopped and took a deep breath, which was enough to silence Buffy as she waited for Willow to speak. "Buffy," she finally said quietly, "I'm storming off. It doesn't really work if you come with me."

"Oh." Her friend looked unhappy, but at least she stayed where she was and let Willow walk away and salvage a little bit of her pride.

Willow was headed up the stairs to class when an unfamiliar voice called out to her. "Uh . . . Willow?"

She stopped, but the girl standing at the bottom of the staircase wasn't someone she knew—slender, with a pretty face framed by stylishly cut dark hair. "Hi."

"Anya," she said, indicating herself. "I'm sort of new here. I, uh, know Cordelia?"

"Ooh," Willow said, intentionally keeping her face expressionless. "Fun."

Anya wasn't dumb. "Yeah, uh—listen," she said, hurrying past the awkwardness. "I have this little project I'm working on, and I heard you were the person to ask if—"

"Yeah, that's me," Willow cut in, her mouth twisting. "Reliable dog geyser person." *Whatever,* she thought. *I might as well get used to it.* "What do you need?"

Anya smiled confidentially at her and gave a furtive glance around, as if to make sure no one was close enough to overhear. "Oh, it's nothing big. Just a little spell I'm working on."

Willow perked up. "A spell? Oooh—I like the black arts."

Anya nodded. "I just need a secondary to create a temporal fold. I heard you were a pretty powerful Wicca, so . . ."

Willow grinned. It was *so* good to have someone need her for a change in a way that meant she was an equal *part* of what was going on, appreciated as opposed to just used or taken for granted. "You heard right, mister," she said brightly. "I'm always ready to work some dark mojo. So tell me," she asked slyly, "is it dangerous?"

"Oh, no," Anya assured her quickly.

Willow was disappointed. "Well . . . could we pretend it is?"

They'd waited until later and slipped into one of the empty classrooms, and now they were almost ready to go. Everything seemed in order—candles, bones, herbs, blessed stones, and dried chicken feet arranged just so on the floor around the object that was the center of the spell, a white china plate with a color rendition of a necklace carefully painted on it.

"The necklace was a family heirloom passed down for generations, then it was stolen from my mom's apartment," Anya told Willow. The dark-haired girl carefully funneled colored sand into a small glass jar as Willow made the final adjustments to the wide line of bones and charms.

"How does the spell work?" Willow asked.

"We both call on Eyrishon, the endless one," Anya said matter-of-factly. The candles flickered in the room, creating the perfect atmosphere for magic. "Offer up the standard supplication. Then there's a teensy temporal fold—we hope. Then I pour the sacred sand on the representation of the necklace, and Eyrishon brings it forth from the time and place where it was lost."

"Cool," Willow said. She liked the way Anya talked to her as if she knew everything. While she'd never done a temporal fold before, she was fairly certain of what to expect and couldn't imagine there would be any problems.

"Of course," Anya added, "there's a lot of theory there, but I figure it's worth a shot. Are we ready?"

Theory? That cast a shiver of doubt over things, but then again, it was only a necklace they were trying to get back. "I think so," Willow said.

Anya settled comfortably onto the floor across from her, separated by the line of candles and charms. At Anya's reassuring smile, they both let their eyes close nearly all the way, and Anya extended her right hand with the palm up. *"Eyrishon. K'shala. Meh-uhn,"* she intoned.

Willow followed suit, holding up her left hand and turning it so that their fingertips met. *"Diprechat,"* Willow said. *"Doh-tehenlo Nu-Eyrishon."*

Anya opened her eyes. "The child to the mother," she said to Willow.

"The river to the sea," Willow responded solemnly.

Anya held out the jar, and Willow wrapped her hand around Anya's, and they both closed their eyes again. "Eyrishon, hear my prayer," Anya whispered.

For a long moment there was nothing. Then light

streamed from somewhere near the ceiling and enveloped them both in an electric-looking swirl. They jerked beneath the power of something unseen in the room, and—

Willow's eyes jolted open.

Images zinged past. People fighting in a huge room filled with broken crates and wood—Giles, a female demon whose face she didn't recognize, Buffy fighting vampires that looked way too much like herself and Xander, ultimately staking Xander into a doubled-over pile of dust. She saw the Master, with his hellishly shriveled face and red, tooth-filled mouth, and, yes, there was a necklace—Anya's?—big and glowing where it lay on a table as someone brought a heavy rock down on top of it—

Caught between the place in her vision and the real world, Willow felt her body shake violently as Anya tried to turn the jar of sand over. She felt herself instinctively resist—

And there was Oz, fighting with a vampire who looked uncomfortably like her, his face bloodied and hair wild as he rushed at the bloodsucker and lifted her toward a piece of wood jutting from the wall—

—but couldn't. Somewhere in her consciousness she knew the sand was falling toward their hands as a thunderclap boomed through the classroom. The sound was huge and jolting, and they both jumped, and for a moment—

—just

—one

—moment

—their fingertips parted.

And the sacred sand cascaded not through their touching hands but only through Willow's outstretched fingers.

—but the vampire who could have been her twin disappeared from within Oz's hold.

Then the light was gone, and the sound was gone, and Willow and Anya broke apart, each gasping.

Willow scrambled backward. "That was—what was *that?*"

She got to her feet, more than a little freaked, but Anya didn't answer. Instead, the other girl went to her knees and searched frantically among the items on the floor. "It's not here—it's not *here!*"

Willow backed up, her breathing still coming fast and frightened. "Okay . . . that's a little blacker than I like my arts."

Still kneeling, Anya only glared at her. "Oh, don't be such a wimp."

"That wasn't just a temporal fold, that was some weird . . . Hell place," Willow protested shakily. "I don't think you're telling me everything!"

"I swear," Anya said through clenched teeth, "I'm just trying to find my *necklace.*"

Willow scowled at her. "Did you try looking inside the sofa from Hell?"

Anya sat back and took a breath, then gave her a tentative smile. "Look, we'll try it again, and if—"

"No! I think emphatically not!"

Anya's expression went indignant. "I can't do it by myself!"

"That's a relief," Willow snapped. She picked up her backpack and shoved her notebooks into it. "I'm *out* of here."

"Fine—go!" Anya spat. "Idiot child."

Willow leaned down. "I believe these chicken feet are mine," she said, insulted. "Magic is dangerous, Anya. It's not to be toyed with." She turned away huffily. "Now, if you'll excuse me, I have someone else's homework to do."

She wasn't quite out the door when she heard Anya's

furious voice. "Nothing!" the other said. *"Nothing!"* Willow glanced over her shoulder, then decided it was best just to keep going when she saw Anya pick up the hand-painted plate and smash it to bits against the floor.

She came to with a hiss of pain and found herself on the floor, the echo of something breaking ringing inside a faraway space in her brain. She knew this place, had been here just a few moments before, but . . . where were all the people? The vampires and the humans had been fighting, there'd been blood and vamp dust everywhere, screams and curses, and it had all been such glorious fun. This . . .

This was *empty*.

And dull—*dull* was a good word for it. There wasn't a soul or soulless person around, and everything was way too peacefully quiet for her liking. Different and . . .

"This is weird," Vamp Willow said.

Her words echoed in the empty room, and she stood and smoothed her clothes—tight red satin corset trimmed with black lace, tighter black leather pants, and heeled platform boots. She might not know where she was or where everyone else had gone, but at least that much hadn't changed. She still had all her strength and senses . . . if she'd wanted it, the rat hiding behind the pile of crates on her left wouldn't have stood a chance. Then another thought occurred to her, and, momentarily nervous, she gave a little mental push and checked her teeth with her tongue; still nice and sharp, pointed in all the right places.

Vamp Willow grinned, just a little bit. That was the best part about being a vampire.

The teeth.

CHAPTER 3

Okay, this was just . . . wrong. *All* wrong.

Eyes hooded to hide her confusion, Vamp Willow
walked down the sidewalk. Everything here was way too
bright—the beautiful night sky was overwhelmed by neon
signs and street lamps and the glow from dozens of shop
windows. Teenagers screamed, but not with fear—they
horsed around and played tug of war with each other, they
talked, they *laughed* until her ears hurt with the sound of
it. Kids ran back and forth, couples sat at the Espresso
Pump and talked while they drank mochas. There were
even *old* people, strolling arm in arm into the blazingly
bright entrance to the movie theater. Where was the terror,
the fear of the night and the creatures that roamed it which
should be leaking out of every disgusting human pore?

"Excuse me, young lady—"

She whirled and found an old lady reaching out a
shriveled hand toward her sleeve. She didn't know—or

care—what Grandma wanted, and she didn't wait to find out. Before the dry fingers could close on her arm, Vamp Willow growled viciously, the lionlike sound of her own warning the only comforting noise for blocks.

"Oh!" the old woman squeaked, and wisely scurried in the opposite direction.

Enough, Vamp Willow thought. If there was one place left that still had to be welcoming for her, it was the Bronze, and she let her booted feet carry her there now. But the scene that greeted her when she pushed through the door was even worse than what she'd found out on the streets of what was supposed to be Sunnydale—the place was warm, disgustingly so, because it was packed to the rafters with humans . . . and every darned one of them was alive.

She'd hoped for a good heavy metal sound; instead the sign at the front door said "K's Choice," and onstage was some blond chick with a mellow voice who wouldn't have lasted a minute had things been the way they *should* have around here. The pinball game blinked merrily while teenagers milled around the red-covered billiard tables apparently without a care in the world. Where were the Master and his minions? Where was the *sanity* in this place? If she could just find—

"Hey!"

Vamp Willow jerked to a stop as a tall, dark-haired boy bumped full force into her, then looked at her in amazement. "Rosenberg? What are you doing—trick-or-treating?"

Instead of answering, she looked him up and down, amazed at how much foolish nerve one small human could have. Somewhere off to the side, her sensitive hearing caught someone call the kid by name—Percy. The name meant nothing to her.

The teen lifted his chin and looked down his nose at

her. "You're supposed to be at home doing my history report," Percy said. He pointed a finger at her and swaggered slightly. "I flunk that class, you're in big trouble with Snyder. Until we graduate, I *own* you."

"Bored now," she said sweetly.

And rammed the heel of her hand into his sternum.

Percy-who-thought-he-owned-her went flying backward, end over end like a spinning beach ball. He came down hard on the floor at the other side, gasping and groaning as he tried to push himself back to his feet.

Tsk-tsk. Too slow.

"I'm having a terrible night," Vamp Willow said in a pouty voice as she ambled over to him. Percy still hadn't made it up—obviously she'd have to help him.

She reached down and wrapped her black-nailed fingers around his throat and pulled him upright, balanced him in front of her while she gave him a seductive smile. "Wanna make it better?" she cooed.

The boy's left hand automatically closed over the one she had gripped around his throat, and he tried to take a swing at her on the right. Useless—she easily blocked it, then only smiled wider as he opted for attempting to choke her in return when his punch fell short. Stupid human child—didn't he know she didn't need air anymore?

"What's going on?" asked a familiar voice from a few feet away. "Is there a funny thing?" Was that her beloved Xander? There was a pause, then she heard him say, "Whoa!"

Percy's hold—puny to begin with—began to weaken as his oxygen-starved lungs tried futilely to work. She was trying to decide whether to continue choking Percy or bite him when someone else leaped into her field of vision and broke their dual hold, sending Percy-boy sprawling and saving him from unconsciousness.

Pity.

"Back off!" the new arrival growled at the cowering Percy. "Stay the hell away from her!"

"Okay," Percy croaked from floor level. "Sure." He scuttled away through the crowd like an oversized crab.

His rescuer turned to face her, and Vamp Willow smiled in delight, her first real happy since she'd found herself in the empty plant. "Xander . . ."

Xander's eyebrows rose as he looked at her, then gestured at her clothes. "Will—changing the look not an idle threat with you."

"You're alive." Pleased, Vamp Willow stepped forward and wrapped her arms around him, felt him automatically hug her in return. He felt good and familiar, and she let her hands move down his back and—

He jerked a little. "Uh, Will . . . this is verging on naughty touching here. We don't want to fall back on bad habits." Without warning, he yanked out of her embrace and grabbed her fingers. "Hands!" he exclaimed. "Hands in new places!"

Her smile went upside down then, and she leaned forward enough to sniff at him. Frowning now, she pulled away and back-stepped. "You're . . . *alive.*"

Xander stared at her. "You mentioned that earlier. Will . . . are you okay?"

"No," she said miserably. She looked around, but she was still stuck in this nightmare place. "Everything's . . . different."

"Xander, there you are."

A girl's voice, someone else familiar and not at all welcome. Vamp Willow hadn't thought she could get any unhappier, but unlife was obviously full of surprises.

"Hey, Buff," Xander said.

"Aren't you going to introduce me to your new—holy God, you're Willow!"

She knew this one, all right—the blond hair and all-American face. Everybody knew her.

Vamp Willow's eyes narrowed. "You . . ." she said in a low voice.

But the Slayer wasn't looking at her as she should be—as the mortal enemy of all vampires. Instead, there was a funny expression on her face—confusion, and something else Vamp Willow couldn't fathom, like a strange desire not to offend her.

"You know what?" Buffy said with false brightness. "I like the look. It's, um, extreme, but it's—it looks good, it's a leather thing, and it's very . . ." She glanced at Xander a little desperately before looking back at Vamp Willow. "I said extreme already, right?"

"I don't like you," Vamp Willow hissed.

Weirdness abounded—the Slayer actually looked hurt. "Will, I—I'm sorry about today," she offered. "You know how my foot likes to live in my mouth, but . . . you really didn't have to prove anything."

Again . . . enough of this. "Leaving now," Vamp Willow said. She turned her back and started to walk away.

"Willow, gotta say I'm not loving the new you," the dreadfully alive Xander called after her. She ignored him and kept going.

There were quick footsteps behind her, then the hated Slayer actually had the gall to tug on her arm. "Willow, wait—"

Vamp Willow spun and let herself change into her natural form, relished the thickening of her brow, the tightening of the skin around her mouth as her teeth elongated and sharpened. *"Get OFF me!"* she snarled.

She left them standing there, staring after her as she stalked away into the comforting blackness of the night.

Vamp Willow felt better outside. Although she was still grouchy, still peeved by this whole backward turn of events, the dark sky was like an old friend, the shadows inviting as she strode briskly down the alley beside the Bronze.

She didn't even mind it when she realized she was being followed.

"Willow Rosenberg?" asked a gravelly voice.

She stopped but didn't turn, although it was a shame the two—yes, there were two—vampires behind her couldn't see the wicked smile that spread across the deep red gloss of her lips. "I'm not supposed to talk to strangers," she said in a little girl voice.

"Then we won't talk," he growled.

They rushed at her, but they never really had a chance.

She took the first one—the one who had yet to open his mouth—out with a perfect side kick to the gut that knocked him back and off his feet. The second one—the talker—tried to grab her while his friend clambered up again, but Vamp Willow tossed him over her shoulder as though he weighed no more than a small sack of potatoes. Then the other guy was up, but she caught him with a spinning back kick and blocked the pathetic punch he tried to aim at her and sent him flying again. When the talker leaped at her a final time, she gave him a round-house kick that would have broken all the ribs in a human; a punch and a couple of blocks, then she snagged his arm and twisted it hard enough to flip him to the ground. While his buddy lay unconscious in a pile of trash, Vamp Willow pinned the talker to the ground with one leather-clad knee and gripped his hand in a vicious wristlock.

"You made me cranky," she purred.

"There's been a mistake," the vampire protested. His voice was thick with pain. "We were sent after a human!"

"Really?" Still holding on, she stroked his fingers idly. "Whom do you work for?"

The vampire's face hardened. "I'm not telling you a thing—"

The sentence ended in a cry of pain as Vamp Willow suddenly yanked one of his fingers backward and broke it. "Whom do you work for?" she asked in a sugar-coated tone.

"Wilkins," the vampire gasped. "The Mayor."

Crack. Another finger broke, and the vampire screamed and contorted on the ground. "Whom do you work for?" she asked again. Her fingers gently crawled around yet another of his.

"You!"

Finally figured it out, huh? She let him go and watched disdainfully as he picked himself up. A few seconds later, his companion crawled stiffly out of the trash and joined them. "Get your friends," she said coldly. "Bring them here. The world's no . . . *fun* anymore, so we're gonna make it the way it was." She let an icy smile slide over her features. "Starting with the Bronze."

CHAPTER 4

The walk from the Bronze to the library was made in silence—along with a big piece of her heart, the ability to express her pain and sorrow had been torn out of Buffy at the sight of Vamp Willow as a vampire back at the Bronze. At her side, Xander just seemed like a tall and gawky primitive robot—a machine with no speech center, no grace or fluid movement . . . just one jerky step after another as he tried to get from one place to the next.

So many times in the past the library had been a place of comfort and refuge, but tonight it gave neither. Even the familiar sight of Giles as he stepped out of his office to greet them didn't help.

"Ah, Buffy," he said. "I thought you were going out tonight, didn't expect . . ." His voice trailed off as they stood by the door, still unable to speak. Buffy could feel the wetness of tears on her cheek, and she knew by Giles's expression that he'd just noticed. She saw Giles's

118

fingers tighten around the book he was holding until his knuckles went white. "What is it?"

The three of them sat on the library stairs, shoulders slumped, expressions blank and shocked. And that was the very same part—the *three* of them—that was so *wrong* about it. They were like a four-part puzzle missing the final piece, or a pie out of which someone had stolen a quarter-sized slice, only to leave the insides of the rest of it bleeding at the wound.

"This isn't real," Xander said dully.

Buffy blinked, but even her eyelids were slow and unresponsive. "I can't feel anything. Arms, legs, or . . . anything."

Giles hung his head and stared at his feet. "She was truly . . . the finest of all of us."

"Way better than me," Xander put in.

Giles nodded. "Much, much better."

Buffy's fingers twisted together. "We just saw her at lunch. How could—"

Xander looked up. "It's all my fault."

Giles frowned. "What makes you say that?"

The teenager shrugged helplessly. "I don't know. Statistical probability?"

"No," Buffy said suddenly. "It's me—I'm the one who called her reliable. She must've gone out and gotten attacked, which she never would have done if I hadn't called her reliable, and now my best friend is—"

"What's going on?"

All three of them jerked as they looked up and saw Willow—the one they'd last seen at school wearing a pink sweater trimmed with white flowers—standing right in front of them.

* * *

Hmmm, Willow thought. *This is weird.*

"Jeez, who died?" she asked jokingly.

They were all staring at her as if she was a walking, talking ghost or something, or as if—

All the funny went running out of her. "Oh God," she said, distressed. "Who *died?*"

Xander leaped to his feet, then rushed at her with a cross waving wildly in one outstretched hand. "Back!" he shouted. "Get back, demon!"

Willow just stared at him, at the cross, then back at him. Thrown, he looked at the cross, then shook it as if it was a can of spray paint with a clogged nozzle. He tried again, shoving the holy object energetically at her face.

She simply stood there, wondering what the heck was going on.

"Willow?" Buffy rose from her spot on the library stairs and came slowly forward. What was that on her cheeks—had she been crying? "You're alive?"

Willow gave her a halting smile. "Aren't I usually?"

Before she could say anything else, Buffy jumped forward and bear-hugged her, making little sad snuffling sounds on the collar of her sweater. Willow opened her mouth to ask what the deal was but got the wind knocked out of her again when Xander joined in, wrapping his arms around both Buffy and Willow and squeezing tightly.

It took a few seconds, but she found just enough air. "I love you guys, too," she managed to squeak. "Okay . . . oxygen becoming an issue—"

They released her then and stepped back, staring at her as though she'd suddenly become encased in gold. Since they still weren't talking, Willow decided to try her luck with Giles. "What's going on with these guy—whoa!"

Okay, hugs from your best pals were one thing, but getting one from the librarian kicked the bizarro meter up to the way-too-intense level. She was still pretty jolted when he let her go. "Oh . . ." he said, as if he'd just realized what he done. "Sorry."

No one said anything, but Buffy reached out and fingered a strand of Willow's hair, her expression amazed and grateful.

"It's . . . nice that you guys missed me." Willow eyed them cautiously. "Say, you all didn't happen to do a bunch of drugs, did you?"

Xander's face was pale. "Will, we saw you at the Bronze." He glanced at the others. "A . . . vampire."

"I am *not* a vampire!" Willow said heatedly. How insulting!

"You are!" Buffy said, then must have heard her own words. "I—I mean, you were . . ." She looked at Giles a little desperately. "Giles, planning on jumping in with an explanation any time soon?"

"Oh," Giles said. "Well, something . . ." He looked around the library. No help there. "Something very strange is happening." Obviously clue-deprived.

They all stared at him, then Xander tilted his head. "Can you believe the Watchers Council let this guy go?"

God, how she *hated* being mortal.

It had been so much more exciting, more *enticing,* when she had slid through the world of humans as Anyanka, delivering retribution to unfaithful lovers and misbehaving men. Now, *that* had been a life. Now all she had was—

This.

Anya sighed and settled onto one of the stools at the Bronze's bar, turning up her lip at a rack of postcards on the counter. Useless scraps of paper—mortals wasted their time on the most ridiculous things. Behind her the jukebox pounded out some alternative music tune, a half-dollar's worth of numbers on the list to fill the gap between the band that had just left and the one that was setting up. The failure of her temporal fold spell earlier in the day and having Willow bail on helping her with a second attempt—well, that just figured.

"What a day," she said grumpily, then realized the bartender, a young guy with a buzz cut and a yellow T-shirt, was standing there. "Give me a beer."

"ID," he said with absolutely no inflection in his voice. She scowled at him. No effect.

"ID"

Anya felt her temper boil over, and she balled up her fists. *"I'm eleven hundred and twenty years old!"* she railed. *"Just give me a friggin' BEER!"*

He just stood there, and absolutely nothing in his expression changed. "ID."

She gave up. "Give me a Coke."

On the stage, Oz grunted as he and Devon struggled to move a heavy amp a little more to the left. "Man," Devon panted. "We need a roadie. Other bands have roadies."

Oz straightened and wiped his hands on his pants. "Other bands know more than three chords," he pointed out. "Your professional bands can play up to six, and sometimes seven, completely different chords."

Devon made a snorting sound. "That's just like . . . fruity jazz bands."

"Oz."

He turned and saw Angel climbing the steps to the stage. "Hey, man. You looking for Buffy?"

The tall vampire inclined his head. "As always."

Oz picked up some of the wires puddled on the stage and began tying them out of the way. "No sightings as of yet, but I think she said she'd show."

Next to him, Devon got that look on his face when he thought—key word, *thought*—he'd just gotten a great idea. "Hey, man, how'd you like to be our roadie?"

"Less than you'd think," Angel said dryly.

"Well, stick around," Oz told Angel. "I'm sure Buffy'll—" He broke off as he followed Angel's suddenly fixed stare to where the back door was just visible from the stage. Was that . . . oh, yeah. A vampire, full vamp face even, was blocking it, clearly intent on keeping everyone *in*. Like Angel's, Oz's gaze immediately went to the other exits, then the front door. Why wasn't he surprised to see a bloodsucker guarding every single one?

"That doesn't look good," Oz said in a low voice.

As if to confirm his words, some guy tried to push past what looked like the ringleader at the front door, and for his trouble he got tossed, hard, on top of the nearest pool table. His date screamed, and voices started rising, then the main vamp stepped forward. "Everybody, *shut up!*" he bellowed.

Oz and Angel exchanged looks and decided to do a wait-and-see right now. "All right," continued the head guy in a harsh voice. "Nobody causes any trouble or tries to leave, and nobody gets hurt."

Angel shifted slightly. "Why don't I believe him?"

"Well, he lacks credibility." Oz raised an eyebrow. "Can you get out of here?"

Angel tilted his head upward briefly. "Skylight in the roof—I can make it."

"I think we need some backup."

Angel didn't look convinced. "I think I'm needed here."

Oz shrugged. "Ten to one—could get pointless." He started to say something else, then shock ran through him, through *all* of him, paralyzing him for one seemingly forever moment. A foot to his right, Angel looked as appalled as Oz felt. Were they seeing what he thought they—? "Get Buffy," he managed to say to Angel. "Do it *now*."

With a last horrified glance over his shoulder, Angel slipped into the shadows behind the amps and began a hand-over-hand climb up the rope that hugged the wall.

"Dude," Devon said from behind him. His voice was very, very quiet, but Oz still could tell his pal was smiling and thought this was mega-cool. If he only knew. "Check out your girlfriend."

Now, this is more like it, Vamp Willow thought as she glided into the Bronze. "Look . . . everybody's all afraid," she said with a sly grin at the humans around her. "It's just like old times." She moved forward, savoring the smell of fear saturating the air. Near the center of the room, she stopped at a table where a pretty girl with dark blond hair sat on a high stool. Vamp Willow smiled at her. "What's your name?"

What a pathetic, scared thing she was, barely able to answer, her eyes huge and wide with terror. "Sandy," she finally got out.

Still smiling, Vamp Willow ran her fingers down Sandy's arm, then took her hand and pulled her to her feet. Too intimidated to resist, Sandy followed where she was led, as though she were Vamp Willow's baby sister. Still holding Sandy's hand, Vamp Willow addressed the crowd as though she were talking to a group of preschoolers. "You don't have to be afraid . . . just to please me. If you're all good boys and girls," she told them, "we'll make you young and strong for ever and ever. We'll have *fun.*"

She pushed Sandy slightly ahead of her, then gave her a playful lick on the side of the neck. Her eyes narrowed. "If you're not . . ." Vamp Willow whipped her head sideways, morphed into vampire mode instantly, and sank her teeth into Sandy's neck.

Enjoying her feast, she was still well aware that someone onstage—one of the band members?—started for her when she bit down, but one of her boys handily stepped into the guy's way and put an end to *that* idea. The girl spasmed, but Vamp Willow held on easily until she was as empty as one of those foil packs of fruit punch, then let her meal drop to the floor like so much discarded trash. She shuddered momentarily—*yummy*—then looked at the crowd from beneath half-closed lids. "Questions? Comments?"

Dead silence.

How appropriate.

Then, "Willow—you don't want to do this."

It was that guy, the cute one with the spiked-out red hair who'd been up on the stage. He'd made it as far as the bottom of the steps, so now she tilted her head and sidled up to him. "I don't?" she asked. "But I'm so . . . *good* at it."

But he only stared at her, his expression full of pain and dismay. "Who *did* this to you?" he demanded.

Now it was Vamp Willow's turn to frown. "I know you," she said. "You're a white hat—how come you're talking to me like we're friends?"

"Because he thinks you're someone else."

Vamp Willow spun and found a pretty young girl with dark hair walking fearlessly toward her. Good old broken-fingered Alphonse started to grab for the stranger, but Vamp Willow stopped him with a slight wave.

"He thinks you're the Willow who belongs in *this* reality," the girl continued.

Vamp Willow considered this. "Another . . . me."

"I'm Anya," the girl said. "You know this isn't your world, right? I mean, you know you don't belong here."

"No . . . this is a *dumb* world." Vamp Willow scowled

at the crowd in general. "In *my* world there are people in chains, and we can ride them like ponies."

"You want to get back there."

"Yeah," Vamp Willow said with a pout.

Now Anya's grin was dark and calculating, and Vamp Willow liked that. A lot. "So do I."

Standing at the far end of the library counter, Willow pressed herself against the wall. This whole herself-as-a-vampire situation made her want to scrunch down and hide—of all the things she'd imagined seeing, had actually *seen*, herself as a bloodsucker was *not* on the I-want-to list.

A shudder worked its way up her spine. "This is creepy," she said. "I don't like the thought that there's some vampire out there who looks like me."

Xander folded his arms. "Not looks like—*is*."

"It's exactly you, Willow, every detail . . . except for your not being a dominatrix . . ." Buffy hesitated. "As far as we know."

Willow smiled ruefully. "Oh, right. Me and Oz play Mistress of Pain every night."

A few feet away, Giles frowned, and both Buffy and Xander looked disturbed. "Did anybody else just go to a scary visual place?" Xander asked slowly.

"Oh, yeah," Buffy said as Giles raised his eyeglasses in agreement.

Willow started to remind them that this was ridiculous when Angel burst through the library doors and hurried up to Buffy. "Buffy, I . . ." He faltered, apparently trying to find the right words. "Something's happened that . . . *Willow's dead.*"

Xander and Buffy both nodded agreeably, then Angel glanced over at her. "Hey, Willow," he said automatically.

He turned back to Buffy, then jerked and looked back at Willow, then turned back to Buffy again. "Wait—"

Xander inclined his head. "We're right there with you, buddy."

"We saw her, too," Buffy told Angel. "At the Bronze."

Angel tried to regroup. "Okay. Well, she's there now—with a cadre of vampires looking to party."

Buffy got hastily to her feet. "Then we can worry about who she is *after* we stop the feeding frenzy."

It took only a few minutes for Willow and the others to get their coats and weapons and head out. "How many were there?" Buffy asked as the group strode out of the library.

Angel thought about this for a moment. "Eight or ten."

Buffy looked to Giles. "Should we call Faith?"

The librarian gave an emphatic shake of his head. "No. I don't want her in combat yet, not around civilians."

"Here, here," Xander said.

"Uh, guys?"

The tone of Willow's voice stopped them, and her friends turned and looked at her expectantly.

"The . . ." She swallowed. "What are we going to do with . . . me? The . . . other me?"

No one answered, then Buffy stepped forward and touched her arm. "I don't know, Will," she said gently. "We just have to stop them."

"I get that," Willow said unhappily. "I just kind of wanted to know—oh!" A thought jumped into her head. "Hey—go! I'll catch up."

She let them start moving away and headed back to the library. Inside, she leaned over the counter, trying to see. It hadn't been used since the last time Oz had broken out on one of his werewolf nights, but if she remembered correctly, what she wanted ought to be right here somewhere—

A cold hand closed over her mouth and yanked her back as an arm, even colder, wrapped around her waist and held her tight. A silky voice, achingly familiar but with an undercurrent of darkness that Willow found completely petrifying, spoke into her ear.

"Alone at last . . ."

CHAPTER 5

"**W**ell, look at me. I'm all . . . *fuzzy*."

Her captor let go, then spun Willow to face her. Horrified, Willow stared at the darker side of herself and tried to find something coherent to say. "What do I want with you? Uh, I mean—"

Her vampire self regarded her from beneath half-closed lids. "Your little schoolfriend, Anya, said that you're the one who brought me here. She said that you could get me back to my world."

"Oh." For a moment, Willow didn't know what she was talking about. Then she remembered the temporal fold spell that Anya had claimed had failed. She winced. "Oh—oops."

Vamp Willow smiled darkly. "But I don't know . . ." She circled, her movements slinky and confident. When she was standing behind her again, she continued. "I kind of *like* the idea of two of us. We could be quite a team . . . *if* you came around to my way of thinking."

Willow cringed. "Would that mean we have to snuggle?"

"What do you say?" her vampire twin asked, then unexpectedly licked Willow's neck. "Wanna be bad?"

Ewwwww! Willow tried to scrunch up her shoulders. "This just can't get any more disturbing!"

Behind her, Vamp Willow growled playfully. *Is she going to bite?*

Willow ducked out from under the vampire's hold and whirled. "Okay—ick! *Ick!* No more—you're really starting to freak me out!" She tried to sidestep in the direction of the library doors, but the vampire moved with her, as if she instinctively knew what Willow would do. But she didn't know *everything*—

Willow snatched Xander's cross off the counter and brandished it, but her efforts got her only a vicious growl from her leather-clad twin. Before she could react, Vamp Willow reached out and slapped it out of her hand, then in one move lifted her and hurled her over the library counter. Willow landed in a heap on the other side, with probably two dozen places in her body screaming in pain.

"You don't wanna play," she heard the vampire say poutily. "I guess I can't force you." Her bloodsucking twin stepped through the doorway and started toward her. "Oh, wait—I *can*."

There—the thing she'd come back to the library to look for! Willow lunged forward and snatched the tranquilizer gun from its spot beneath the counter, aimed it at herself—her *other* self—and squeezed the trigger.

Vamp Willow looked at her in astonishment, then down at the dart embedded in her stomach. "Bitch," she said nastily.

She collapsed.

* * * *

"It's extraordinary," Giles said.

Willow had caught up with Buffy and the others outside and called them back, and now she watched Angel drag the vampire version of herself into the cage. *Extraordinary,* however, was *not* the word she would have used for the situation.

"It's *horrible,*" she said. "That's me as a vampire? I'm so . . . evil. And skanky." She glanced at Buffy in dismay. "And . . . and I think I'm kind of gay."

Buffy gave her a look that tried to be comforting. "Just remember—a vampire's personality has nothing to do with the person it was."

Angel looked over from where he and Xander were standing at the now-locked door of the cage. "Well, actually," he began, then his words sputtered out at Buffy's hard look and Willow's wide eyes. "Uh . . . that's a good point."

"What do we do now?" Xander asked.

"We still have to get to the Bronze," Giles noted.

Angel nodded. "Even if they're supposed to wait for her, they might start feeding—vampires are not notoriously reliable."

Xander gave them all a lopsided grin. "So we charge in, much in the style of John Wayne?"

Giles clearly wasn't big on the idea. "High casualty risk. I haven't any other plan, though."

Buffy chewed on her lip for a second, then held up her hand and gave Willow a little I'm-sorry-in-advance smile. "I have a really . . . bad idea."

The alley by the side of the Bronze was never her favorite place in the world. Tonight, Willow found it even less so.

Angel jumped down from atop the Dumpster where he'd been peering through a high window and into the

Bronze. "They're still in a holding pattern." He looked at her. "That's good—it means they must really be afraid of you."

"Who wouldn't be?" Willow indicated her outfit and tried to smile, but this . . . *thing* she was wearing—corset, piece of torture clothing, whatever they called it—seemed bent on curbing most of her muscular abilities. Never in the world would she have imagined herself in black leather and red satin.

Buffy must have picked up on her discomfort. "You okay in that?"

"It's a little . . . binding," Willow said. A corner of her mouth lifted. "I guess vampires really don't have to breathe." She squirmed, trying to get the folds and curves properly in place, then glanced down automatically. *Yikes . . . cleavage.* "Gosh," she said without thinking. "Look at those."

For a moment they all froze, accidentally doing exactly that. Then Giles cleared his throat. "Willow, you go in and defuse the situation as best you can. At least get some of them to come outside, even the odds a bit."

She nodded hesitantly, and Buffy put a comforting hand on her arm. "First sign of trouble, you give us the signal. We'll come in hard and fast."

Xander glanced from Buffy to Willow. "What's the signal?"

"Me screaming." Willow found a sickly smile.

Angel stepped forward. "Giles, you and Xander wait by the back entrance."

"Right." The two of them moved quickly into the shadows as Buffy studied Willow. "You sure you're up to this?"

"Don't worry," she told her friend. "I won't do anything that could be interpreted as brave."

"We'll be right outside," Buffy assured her.

By all accounts that should have made Willow feel better, but that disappeared as soon as Buffy and Angel faded back and into the darkness. She took a deep breath, then knocked on the side entrance. It was opened by a vampire, big and super ugly enough to shoot fear through every nerve in her body.

No—she mustn't lose it.

"Hi," she said. "I'm back."

Her tone was a little on the cutesy edge, and he looked at Willow doubtfully but moved aside as she stepped forward, struggling mightily not to trip in the high-heeled platform boots and nearly doing so anyway on the doorjamb. Then he was closing the door behind her, cutting off her escape route. She glanced around the room, trying to look convincingly evil, then saw another, bigger vampire approach . . . along with, wonder of wonders, Anya.

"Did you find the girl?" the vampire grated.

The girl—he must be talking about the other her. "Yep," she said. "I did." Hmmm, her tone was still perhaps a little too bright here, not nearly mean and nasty.

"Where is she?" Anya asked eagerly.

What was Anya's part in this—had she sent Vamp Willow after her? Of course she had, but why? "I . . . killed her," Willow said, then hesitated, trying to figure out why the other girl looked so distressed. "And sucked her blood, as we vampires do." She peered around, then glided up to the vamp who'd let her in a few seconds ago. "You know, I think maybe I heard something out there. Why don't you go check?"

He obeyed as Willow turned her attention back to Anya and the vampire who was apparently, next to Willow herself, the one in charge. "How could you kill her?" Anya demanded now. "She was our best shot at getting your world back!"

Uh-oh. Okay, her story had run afoul of some plan she hadn't known about, but she'd just have to cover. Willow pasted on her best scowl and circled Anya the same way Vamp Willow had circled her. "I don't like that you dare question me," she said ominously. "Maybe I'll . . . have my minions take you out back and kill you horribly." She came back around, locking eyes with Oz as she passed, then chancing a tiny smile and hidden wave. Relief flashed across his expression, and warmth filled her—he must have been scared plenty earlier when he saw the vampire version of Willow.

"Vampires," Anya said in disgust. "Always thinking with your teeth."

Willow glowered at her and made her expression petulant. "She . . . bothered me," she said, slowly working her way toward another of the guard-type bloodsuckers stationed here and there. "She's so weak and accommodating. It's pathetic . . . she's always letting people walk all over her, and then she gets cranky at her friends for no reason." She shrugged, momentarily enjoying the role of spoiled royalty. "I just couldn't let her live." She stopped by another young vampire and patted him on the shoulder companionably. "You know, he's been gone for a while," she noted with a nod toward the side door. "Why don't you check on him?" With luck, he'd end up staked by Buffy and Angel, as the first one had no doubt been.

When she turned back, Anya was watching the guard leave with a perplexed expression, and the ringleader vampire was facing Willow. "Well, boss," he rasped. "Since that plan is out, why don't we get on with the killing?"

Vamp Willow came to lying on the floor, as though she'd had nothing better in the world to do than take a nap. For a second she stretched, then realized that something was wrong—*really* wrong—with what she was wearing. And when she looked down . . .

Pink and fuzzy.

"Oh," she growled softly. "This is like a nightmare." And it got worse when she realized she was inside the library cage—*locked* inside.

"Hello—Giles?"

Vamp Willow jerked, then rose to see who was calling out in that sugary-sweet voice. A girl—tall and dark-haired, dressed to kill in a tight black and silver sparkling dress and high heels the way human women sometimes did. Wait . . . she knew this person—

"Wesley?" the teenager asked with considerably more hope in her tone. Vamp Willow saw her look toward the librarian's office and quickly pat a stray curl back into place. "I just happened to stop by . . . for books."

Vamp Willow eyed the girl from behind the metal gate. "Hey, you."

The teenager whirled in surprise, then saw her and came forward. "Hey, *me?*" she repeated, obviously insulted. "Hey, me, *what?* I have a name, you know."

Vamp Willow searched her memory. "Uh . . . Cordelia."

The other girl looked at her disdainfully. "What'd you do—lock yourself in the book cage?"

"Yeah," Vamp Willow said. "Let me out." She hesitated, trying to find the right act. "Cuz I'm so . . . helpless." *Hmmm . . . was that convincing enough?*

Cordelia looked at her blankly, then shrugged. "Okay." She went over and started hunting around behind the library counter. "I think Giles keeps a spare—ah." She picked up the set of keys lying next to the computer. "How'd you manage to lock yourself in, anyway?"

Vamp Willow paced restlessly behind the locked door.

"I was . . . looking at the books." What else should she say to keep up the charade? "I like books, because I'm so . . . shy."

"Yeah, *right*," Cordelia said sarcastically. "The famous shy girl act all the boys fall for." She came back to the door and sorted through the keys until she found the right one.

"Open the cage," Vamp Willow coaxed, ready to—

"Wait," Cordelia said.

Vamp Willow froze. Uh-oh . . . had Cordelia realized that the Willow she was talking to wasn't the Willow she thought she knew?

Cordelia stepped back, keys still annoyingly separated from the lock. "It occurs to me that we've never really had the opportunity to talk. You know, woman to woman." The pretty teen arched an eyebrow. "With you locked up."

Vamp Willow ran a hand down the cold metal of the door mesh. "Don't wanna talk," she said slowly. "Hungry."

But Cordelia only ignored her. "What could we talk about?" she said thoughtfully. Suddenly, she put on an expression of exaggerated brightness. "Hey—how about the ethics of boyfriend stealing?"

"I don't know if I . . . *feel* like killing anymore," Willow said, trying desperately not to sound nervous. This leather corset was so tight she could barely breathe, which was probably a good thing since she was supposed to be masquerading as her vampire self, and vampires weren't supposed to hyperventilate when they were afraid. "I'm so bored," she continued. She passed a girl sitting at a table and ran her hand through the girl's hair, trying to act like Vamp Willow would. Instead of looking sensuous, her fingers got stuck in a tangle and pulled; the poor girl was so petrified she didn't move a muscle while Willow freed her hand and moved on. She ambled through the crowd, trying not to feel self-conscious beneath Oz's penetrating gaze. "It would be like . . . shooting fish in a barrel," she finally said. "Where's the fun?"

The ringleader vampire lifted his chin. "With all due respect, boss—the fun would be the eating."

She floundered for a moment, trying to think of a comeback. "Maybe we should let everyone go and . . . give them a thirty-second head start—"

"Wait a minute," Anya said. Realization slid over her features.

"No," Willow interrupted, trying to put anger in her voice. "I like *my* plan!"

Anya rolled her eyes. "Oh, nice try."

"Okay," Willow said hastily. "Let's get to the killing." She pointed at Anya. "Why don't we start with *her?*"

Anya wasn't the least bit intimidated. "Why don't we start with *you?*" She glanced at the vampire standing next to her, then sneered at Willow. "If she's a vampire, I'm the Creature from the Black Lagoon!"

"And okay," Cordelia continued, "it isn't even as if I was that attracted to Xander, it was more just that we kept being put into these life-or-death situations, and that's *always* all sexy and stuff. I mean, I more or less knew he was a loser, but that doesn't make it okay for *you* to come along and—what?"

Vamp Willow said nothing, just stared longingly at the girl's neck from where she was, *still*, imprisoned in the book cage.

"Do I have something on my neck?" Cordelia demanded.

"Not yet . . ." Vamp Willow said tiredly. Wasn't she ever going to shut up?

Cordelia strained to look down at her shoulder. "Am I getting a zit?"

"Cordelia," Vamp Willow said, and this time she didn't have to act to sound as if she was pleading. She was ready to say anything if it would just get her out of this little jail . . . or at least get this girl to be quiet. "I'm very sorry—I realize I was wrong. I'll never steal your boyfriend again."

"As if you *could*." Cordelia pressed her lips together but finally came forward with the key. "I *should* just leave you in there. But I'm a great humanitarian, and you'll just have to think of a way to pay me back sometime."

At last Vamp Willow heard the tumblers turn over, and the hateful door swung open. "Okay," she said happily as she stepped out and faced her rescuer. She raised her head and let her face slide into natural vampire mode, then gave Cordelia a nice, toothy smile. "How about dinner?"

CHAPTER 6

Cordelia screamed loud enough, she thought, to wake the dead.

Oh—wait. A dead thing—as in a vampire Willow—is already awake . . . and chasing me.

She careened out of the library at full speed, with the Willow beast right behind her. Down the hall, turning here, through a doorway there, another hall, then she was in a classroom and weaving through the desks, turning them over behind her in a desperate effort to slow down the creature that followed her. No good— Vamp Willow moved like a cat, or maybe a snake— easily slipping past whatever Cordy tumbled into her path.

"I—I didn't mean all that stuff I said before," Cordelia cried. Her words tumbled out. "I *want* you to have Xander. My blessings on you both—"

The Willow thing grinned at her, showing sharp white

teeth that were surprisingly clean and well cared for. "I'm *so* over him. I need fresh blood."

She lunged forward, but Cordy dodged, screamed again, and barreled through the exit door at the other end of the classroom. More headlong rushing through the halls of Sunnydale High—jeez, it seemed they were forever running around in here, for one reason or another. Then—

Oh, *bad* choice.

She was trapped.

Cordelia spun back to find Vamp Willow striding around the corner. "No more hiding," the vampire said evilly. She didn't even hurry as she moved forward and reached out—

—and Wesley stepped between her and Cordelia.

"Back!" he yelled. He pushed a wooden cross toward Vamp Willow's snarling face. "Creature of the night, leave this place!"

Vampire Willow back-stepped, but only a little. "Don't wanna," she said in a sulky voice. Her gaze flitted hungrily between the cross and Cordelia.

For a second Wesley looked confused, then he pressed his lips together and dug a vial of holy water out of the inside pocket of his suit jacket. He raised it threateningly, and this time Vamp Willow looked as if she was reconsidering. "Whatever," she finally said, obviously ticked off. She turned and stalked away.

Wesley stayed where he was, then crept up to the corner to make sure she was really gone. After a second, Cordelia moved up behind him and lightly touched his back.

"Arghgghghggh!"

She jumped back. "Oh—sorry."

Wesley drew in a ragged breath when he saw it was her and tried to pull himself together. "No—no, a little on edge," he said in that tight British accent. "You know—

men in combat." He made a little growling sound in his throat. "Grrrr. Are . . . you all right?"

"You saved my life!" She saw her chance and went for it, throwing her arms around him and holding on tight. "Oh, thank you!"

For a moment, he returned her embrace, then seemed to remember where—and who—he was. "Yes—yes, well." He pulled away from her, then frowned and looked toward the door. "Was that . . . ?"

Cordelia nodded sadly. "Willow. They got Willow." She gave it a moment of silence, then smiled charmingly at him. "So, are you doing anything tonight?"

Anya and the vampire—Willow had heard someone call him Alphonse—were slowly converging on her. "I am just *so* tired of being around human beings and all their garbage—I don't care if I ever get my powers back." Anya hugged herself and sent Willow a cranky glance. "I think he should eat *you.*"

"This girl has a history of mental problems dating back to early childhood," Willow said hotly. "I'm a bloodsucking fiend!" When they still didn't seem convinced, Willow gestured at the black and red getup she was wearing. "Look at my outfit!"

Alphonse shook his head. "A human—I should have smelled it right away."

Uh-oh. Time for drastic measures. "A human?" Willow demanded. "Oh, yeah? Could a human do this?"

She screamed as loud as she could.

Anya and Alphonse looked at each other. Alphonse shrugged. "I'd say yeah, a human could do that."

"Uh-huh," Anya said at the same time. "Most humans could, yeah."

They turned to look at Willow. The hulking Alphonse

started forward, then—thank goodness—Buffy and Angel burst through the front door and the battle began.

Buffy and Alphonse went at it, exchanging vicious blows as Angel began pummeling the vamps by the counter. An instant later Willow saw Giles and Xander crash through the back entrance; Xander grabbed the nearest bloodsucker, and the librarian lunged in for the kill with a handy swipe of his stake. Customers ran in every direction, some fleeing out the now unguarded entrances, others cowering beneath the pool tables.

Anya must have decided it was time to leave, too, because she turned to run, then jerked to a stop directly in front of Willow. Willow glared at her, then drew her fist back and punched the girl solidly in the nose.

Anya crumbled, then Willow realized just how badly that had hurt. "Ow—ow! It's all happy but *ow!*"

Suddenly Oz was there and pulling her up onto the stage, where Devon had abandoned his hiding place behind the drum set and was now trying to climb the ropes to the skylight as he'd seen Angel do. "Come on," Oz urged. "Devon, let's go!"

Realizing he wasn't going to make it, Devon half fell to the floor, then scrambled after Willow and Oz toward the back door. They'd almost gotten there—

—when the vampire version of herself marched through it and tossed Oz into Devon as if Oz was a bowling ball and his band partner was the pin. On the floor below, Buffy and the others were still energetically fighting the good fight.

Willow faced the darker version of herself and swallowed. "No more snuggles?"

Vampire Willow tackled her, and Willow went down. She tried, but her struggles were pretty useless against the strength of her darker self—in less than two seconds the vampire had wrapped her hands around Willow's throat and was trying to strangle her.

Her vision was tumbling around wildly, and she was running out of air, but out of the corner of her eye, Willow saw Buffy glance her way and realize what was happening. She hit another vampire, then backstabbed with the pool cue; before Alphonse's dust had even fallen to the floor she'd broken the cue in half across the face of another vamp and leaped up onto the stage. She hefted it, then rammed the sharp end of the pool cue toward Vampire Willow's back—

"Buffy, *no!*"

—and stopped it an inch away at Willow's cry.

Her friend hauled the vampire up and arm-locked her. Vampire Willow started to struggle, then realized that what was left of her mini-army was either dead or had hightailed it. Defeat flashed across her face.

"Nice reflexes," Willow said to Buffy as she got up.

Buffy gave her a little smile. "Well, I work out."

Willow turned to her dark twin, who just looked morose. "This world's no fun."

Incredible as it might seem, Willow could relate. "You noticed that, too?"

They were all in the abandoned plant where the vampire version of herself had said she'd woken up. Willow had her own clothes back—thank goodness—and, with a grouchy expression on her face, Anya finished up the preparations for a returning spell under Giles's watchful eye.

Willow smiled to herself as she saw Xander sidle up to Vampire Willow. "So," he said in a gloating tone, "in your reality I'm like this bad-ass vampire, huh? People are afraid of me?"

Her vampire twin gave him a withering look and said nothing.

"Oh, yeah," Xander said, and swaggered away. "I'm bad."

"I'm not sure about releasing this thing into the wild, Will," Buffy said at her side. "It *is* a demon."

She knew this—oh, how she did. "I just can't . . . kill her."

Buffy was silent for a moment. "No," she finally said. "Me, neither."

"I mean, I know she's not me—we have a big nothing in common—but still . . ."

"There but for the grace of getting bit," Buffy said softly.

Willow studied herself from across the circle of magic being worked out on the floor. "We send her to her world, she has a chance. It's the way it should be, anyway."

"I think we're about ready here," Giles said from the floor. Oz leaned over and added something to the circle, then scooted back. Giles gave Anya a sharp look. "Don't you try any tricks, Anyanka, dear."

"I don't need tricks," Anya said sullenly. "When I have my powers back, you will all grovel before me."

Willow made a dismissive sound, then realized Vamp Willow had made exactly the same noise, at the same time.

"If you Willows would complete the circle . . ." Giles instructed.

Willow started to sit where she'd been told, then she turned back to her twin. "Good luck," she offered. "Try not to kill people." They stared at each other for a second, then Willow gave in to the impulse to hug her—after all, she was kind of like a sister, only the bad one in the family. After a moment's hesitation, the vampire returned the embrace.

Willow jerked. "Hands!" she admonished. *"Hands!"*

Before joining the magic circle, Vampire Willow only gave her a sweet and wicked smile.

* * *

Vampire Willow blinked, then realized the plant was no longer abandoned. Humans and vampires ran in every direction, screaming and fighting and, she thought, generally having a grand old time. She grinned widely, then felt herself lifted up in the air. Oz's face flashed in front of her, then she felt something sharp and wooden stick her smack in the middle of her back as he shoved her, hard, against a broken two-by-four that was jutting from the wall frame behind her.

Bull's-eye.

"Oh, fi—" she started to say.

Dust.

EPILOGUE

It's funny, Willow thought, *how everything, or everyone, can look so . . . normal on the surface and have this whole evil side that no one knows anything about.*

"Want to go out tonight?" Buffy asked from beside her.

They were sitting on a bench outside the high school, waiting for the bell to ring. It was a beautiful day—sunny, warm, and filled with happy, laughing students rushing from class to class around them.

Willow, however, didn't feel happy at all. "Strangely, I feel like staying at home. And doing my homework. And flossing. And dying a virgin."

Buffy gave her a sidelong glance. "You know, you can OD on virtue."

Willow wasn't swayed. "Between me and my evil self, I have double guilt coupons. I see now where the path of vice leads—she messed up *everything* she touched. I don't ever want to be like that."

A shadow fell over them, and when Willow lifted her head she saw Percy standing there. "Hey, uh, hi," he said.

Percy . . . and the history paper. Drat. "Oh, hi, Percy." Inwardly Willow winced. "Listen, I didn't have a chance to—"

"Okay," he said, cutting her off, "so I did the outline for the paper on Roosevelt." He thrust a piece of paper at her. "It turns out there were two President Roosevelts, so I didn't know exactly which I was supposed to do . . . so I did both." He held out another sheet of paper. "And I know they're kind of short, but I can flesh them out. Oh, and here's my bibliography."

Speechless, Willow accepted yet a third piece of paper as Percy shuffled his feet uncomfortably. "And I can re-type that if you want," he offered. "You just let me know what I did wrong, and—and I'll get on that." He turned and hurried away, leaving Willow to sit and stare at the completed schoolwork in amazement.

She started to say something to Buffy, then realized Percy had come back. He leaned over and carefully placed a shiny red apple atop the papers on her lap, then took off again.

Willow and Buffy sat there without speaking for a few moments. Finally, Buffy asked, "You want to go out tonight?"

Willow looked at the apple, then to where Percy was hurrying away. "Nine sound good?"

DAILY JOURNAL ENTRY:

This time I don't *dare* let my computer journal get too far behind, otherwise I'll never be able to catch up. Stuff is happening at such a brain-spinning pace I'm afraid I'll forget to record something important, and who else writes this stuff down anyway? Well, maybe Giles, but just think of how it probably reads (and don't forget to add that proper Brit accent), full of Latin demonic references, howevers, wherefores, and who knows what kind of other phrases he learned from the Watchers Council.

Okay, the big major-mondo Bad Thing of the Moment—well, not just the *moment,* but this'll sure get your suspenders in a twist:

Faith has become what they call a Rogue Slayer.

We'd never heard of such a thing, but she's sure writing the book for it. It turns out she's working for that horrid Mayor Wilkins—she's like *his* Slayer! Who would've thought something like this would happen? She mucked everything up even worse by trying to use a demon spell to bring Angel's bad side out again . . . but not before she tried to use boyfriend-stealing tactics that didn't work. Still, it put a big strain on things between Buffy and Angel, and even now things aren't quite the same. Faith tried to blame Buffy for the way she turned out—*bad*—but she made her own choices. She didn't have to walk the dark path, and being the second Slayer in town didn't push her in that direction.

Still, we did discover that the Mayor is planning this thing called the Ascension and that whatever that is happens on Graduation Day. Giles found out that the last time there was one of these Ascension thingies, an entire town was wiped out—fun, huh? Like making it through four years of high school isn't challenging enough. The Mayor, who has managed to make himself invincible, even has a set of instruction books for this big hoopla, although we haven't been able to get our hands on them yet.

Faith's still out there doing God knows what to help the Mayor's Ascension plans come along—like I said, I wish we knew what she was up to. I just can't believe she'd turn to the bad side like that. I mean, we all have to make decisions, you know? We all have our special qualities to help with the never-ending struggle that's all things Sunnydale. Even Xander pitches in with...uh...stuff. I've got my Wiccan powers, which, okay, are not so strong yet, but they're getting there and growing all the time. Faith is a *Slayer*—she has so much strength and power that could be used for good. Jeez, if I could take a quarter of what she has and turn it into a spell that would help Buffy and Giles keep Sunnydale from being sucked up by the Hellmouth, who knows how much progress we'd make?

Sometimes the smallest things can tip the balance in your favor and make all the difference in the world, and it really scares me that Faith's decision to go bad might be the thing that screws up the balance of good and evil here in town.

I mean, if it is, what can we, or I, or anyone do to even things out again?

/PRESS ENTER TO SAVE FILE/

FILE: CHOICES

PROLOGUE

Even for the Mayor, she didn't like this "keep your eyes closed" business. After all, how could you know what to do next if you couldn't see what was happening?

"All right, you can open them now," Mayor Wilkins said.

Faith opened her eyes and found a box in front of her. She was sitting on the Mayor's chair, behind the Mayor's desk—she even had a plate of the Mayor's favorite cookies on her left. And now this—a nice long rectangular box, ruby red and closed up tight with a white taffeta ribbon and bow. Life just couldn't get much better.

"Fab," she said, pleased. "What's the occasion?"

"Faith," he admonished. "As if I need a reason to show you my affection." He moved to one of the chairs and sat, careful not to wrinkle his meticulously pressed suit. "Or my appreciation for running a small errand at the airport."

Her fingers picked at the ribbon, then she stopped. *Fig-*

ures. "Airport? What's next—you gonna want me to help a buddy of yours move a sofa?"

"This isn't a free ride here, young lady," Mayor Wilkins said sternly. "You know, I'm beginning to think somebody's getting a leeetle spoiled." He leaned forward and reached for the gift. "Maybe I should just take this back."

Before he could grasp it, Faith slipped the box onto her lap. "Sorry," she said quickly. He looked at her, waiting. "Sir."

After a moment, his expression softened, and he picked up the platter of cookies and held it out. "That's my girl. Another cookie?" She obeyed without hesitation.

"Now," he said, settling back. "A package is arriving tomorrow night from Central America, something—and I can't *stress* this enough—something *crucially* important to my Ascension. Without it . . ." He gestured at the cookies. "Well, what would Tollhouse cookies be without the chocolate chips?"

Faith chewed on her bite of cookie and considered this. *Not much.*

"A pretty darn big disappointment, I can tell you," the Mayor agreed. Suddenly he switched gears. "Open your present."

Now that she had the go-ahead, Faith brought the box back up to the desktop and ripped into it, making short work of the pretty white ribbon. When she lifted the lid, Faith was so stunned that for a long five seconds all she could do was look at what was inside.

"There," Mayor Wilkins said happily. "That look on your face is my reward."

She lifted the gift from the box and held it up. It was a heavy, intricately cut and carved hunting knife with a black bone handle and curved spikes close to the hilt.

She'd never owned anything remotely like it. "This is a thing of *beauty*, boss."

Wilkins nodded. "Well, it cost a pretty penny, so you just take good care of it. And you be careful not to put somebody's eye out with that thing." He came around and pulled a roll of plastic wrap out of a desk drawer, then fussily covered up the plate of cookies. "Until I tell you to."

Faith turned the knife so that it caught the glimmer of the lamps around the room, then she gave him a dark, dark smile. "Got any particular eyes in mind?"

Oh, nasty, Buffy thought.

This one was a woman, and she looked worse than most—maybe she'd been really, really old when she'd been turned, but then who, and why, had the sire bloodsucker bothered?

In the meantime, the creature came at her again, snarling and wrinkle-faced, with long black hair slightly streaked with gray. She caught it with a hard roundhouse kick and sent it careening backward—

—right into Angel.

The vamp's bowling ball effect knocked her boyfriend off his feet in the midst of his own struggle with another bloodsucker, this one a younger guy who was still reeling from Angel's last punch. Buffy winced. "Sorry, honey!"

On the ground, Angel blinked. "That's okay." He twisted and flipped the lady vampire, then staked her before she could wriggle away. As her younger companion turned on Buffy, he found himself in a glad-to-meetcha moment with Mr. Pointy that slammed him back against a tomb and sent him straight into Dustland.

Hmmmmm, Buffy thought. Older woman and younger guy . . . mother and son? "Well, there's something you don't see every day," she said. Actually, that wasn't really true. "Unless, of course, you're me."

"That was bracing," Angel said as he stood and joined her. "You want to do another sweep?"

A corner of her mouth turned down. "It's what I live for. Sad to say."

He glanced at her. "You too tired?"

"No. It's just . . ." She looked at the ground, then at Angel. "Do you get the feeling that we're kind of in a rut?"

"A rut?"

"You never take me anyplace new." She sounded like a sulky little girl, even to her own ears. Too bad—she was leading up to something bigger here.

But Angel only looked confused. "What about that fire demon nest in the caves near the beach? I thought that was a nice change of pace."

Not exactly what she'd been hoping for. "So this is our future?" she asked. "I mean, this is how we're going to spend our nights when I'm fifty and you're . . ." She cringed. ". . . the exact same age you are now?"

Something growled heavily in the bushes a few feet away, the familiar leonine sound of a vampire about to attack.

Angel stared in that direction. "Let's just get you to fifty."

Another growl. "Liking that plan," Buffy agreed.

Resigned, she and Angel went back into the night's battle.

CHAPTER 1

Now, this was a good way to start the morning. Nice, sunshiny day, juice, toast—even the fact that she had to go through her Earth Sciences book and try to pick up on last night's missed homework didn't bother her so much. If only all the mornings could start like thi—

"Buffy?"

Oops.

"When were you going to tell me?" Joyce asked as she came into the kitchen.

Reluctantly, Buffy reached to take off the earrings she was wearing. "All right, busted. I didn't think you'd notice them."

But her mother only held up a thick-looking envelope. "You were accepted to Northwestern University?" Joyce reached over and hugged her enthusiastically. "Honey, I'm so *proud* of you—that's wonderful!"

"Right," Buffy said. "It's . . . wonderful."

But her mother's face was radiant with happiness. "I mean, it's not cheap, but I know we can make it work if your father pitches in. Not that Northwestern is your only option. It's a great school, though." Joyce looked at the envelope in her hand and smiled even wider. "I'm so proud of you."

"You said that before."

Joyce nodded and gazed at her. "And will again soon."

"Mom," Buffy began. "You know I can't . . ." She couldn't finish, couldn't bear to crush the hopeful expression on her mom's face. She knew she should be honest and just say it, get it all out in the open right now—

She bailed.

"I just can't decide on a school right now," Buffy heard herself say. "I just have to, you know, sleep on it. Mull it over, raise them up on my inner flagpole and see which one I salute."

Joyce squeezed her arm. "Oh, I know, sweetheart. I'm just so pleased you have so many choices." She sat up straighter as something occurred to her. "Oooh, your Aunt Arlene and her family live in Illinois—I've got to call and tell them." She took the envelope and went to the phone.

Buffy stood and gathered up her bag and books. She'd only taken two steps when—

"Oh, Buffy?"

She stopped and faced her mother, who'd tucked the phone between her head and her shoulder while she dialed. "I know—you're proud of me."

Joyce raised one eyebrow. "Don't forget to put my earrings back in my dresser before you go out."

Rats.

As she headed up the stairs, her mother's conversation followed her, digging in as she went.

"Arlene? It's Joyce—hi, how're you doing? You're

never going to believe where Buffy got accepted to school . . ."

Snyder's mouth twisted as he walked briskly across the Quad on the way to his office. It was lunchtime, and students dawdled everywhere, sprawling on the grass, slouching at the tables, leaning against the trees—they were like an infestation, for crying out loud. An invasion of out-of-control pests. If he had his way, he'd run this place like a military academy—

Ah-ha!

There, at a picnic table and right in front of him, without even trying to hide it, a boy in a white shirt joined a pal and handed over a brown paper bag. No time to waste—Snyder marched over and snatched the bag out of the other teen's hand. "Okay, what's in the bag?" he demanded.

The boy who'd been about to open it—Snyder mentally labeled him "Red" because of the red sweater he was wearing—gaped at him, putting on a good act of confusion. "My lunch."

The principal curled his lip. "Is that the new drug lingo?"

The two kids stared at him as if he was crazy. "No," insisted Red. "It's my lunch."

Ignoring him, Snyder pulled the top of the bag open and peered into it.

Sandwich wrapped in plastic, an orange, a couple of oatmeal raisin cookies in a Baggie. Darn it, he couldn't even fault it for being unhealthy.

Without a word he handed the bag back to Red, then turned to go. The other boy was leaning away from him at the table, practically tilting over. "Sit up straight," Snyder snapped.

He stalked off, watchful eyes on them all. The kids

were everywhere, and so were the drugs and who knew what else.

And he wasn't one to let down his guard.

Across the lawn, Willow saw Principal Snyder lording it over a couple of guys at another table. She watched for signs that he was headed their way, but after doing something to the lunch bag one of the guys had, Little Rat Man took off in the other direction. Thank goodness for tiny favors.

Oz sat next to her at the table, his arm across her shoulders, and Willow returned her attention to Buffy's story about her conversation with Joyce at breakfast. "Sounds like your mom's in a state of denial."

Buffy smiled thinly. "More like a continent. She just has to realize I can't go away."

"Well, maybe not now," Willow said. "But soon. Maybe." When Buffy only looked at her, Willow flinched. "Or maybe I, too, hail from Denial Land."

Buffy shrugged. "U.C. Sunnydale—at least I got in." She brightened considerably. "But you—I can't believe you got into Oxford!"

Willow inhaled. "It's pretty exciting."

"You're into some deep academia there," Oz noted.

Buffy grinned. "That's where they make Gileses."

"I know! I could learn and have scones." She faltered a bit. "Although I don't know how I feel about going to school in a foreign country."

"Everything in life is foreign territory," Xander said from his spot under a tree a few feet away. He sounded far, far wiser than he actually was. He held up the book he was reading, *On the Road.* "Kerouac," he informed them. "That's my teacher. The open road is my school."

Buffy snickered. "Making the open Dumpster your cafeteria."

Xander sniffed. "Go ahead, mock me."

"I think she just did," Oz said blandly.

"We Bohemian, antiestablishment types have always been persecuted," Xander said defensively.

"Well, sure," Oz replied. "You're all so weird."

"I think it's neat," Willow put in, "you doing the backpack, trail mix, happy wanderer thing."

Xander actually seemed proud of himself. "I'm aware it scores kind of high on the hokey meter, but I think it'll be good for me. Help me to find myself."

"And help us to lose you," Cordelia's acid voice cut in. "Everyone's a winner."

Willow and the others looked up at the brunette as she stopped between Xander's tree and their table. Xander closed his book. "Well, look who just popped open a fresh can of venom," he said, just as caustically. "Hey, Cordy—hear about Will getting into Oxnard?"

"Oxford," Willow corrected automatically.

"And M.I.T. and Yale and every other college on the face of the planet?" Xander added. "As in your face I rub it." He looked absurdly pleased with himself, and Willow could have smacked him for starting this. Where else could it lead but to bad?

As expected, Cordy took the bait and ran with it. "Oxford—whoopie. Four years in Tea Bag Central sounds thrilling. And M.I.T. is a Clearasil ad with housing, and Yale's a dumping ground for people who didn't get into Harvard." She sent Willow a haughty look.

Bait was one thing, but then there was true ammunition. "I got into Harvard," Willow protested gently.

That threw Cordy just enough for Xander to recoup. "Any clue what college you might be attending?" he asked his former girlfriend. "So we can start calculating minimum safe distance?"

"None of your business," Cordelia said sharply. "Certainly nowhere near *you* losers."

Buffy folded her arms. "Don't forget to breathe between insults, you guys."

Cordelia sent Buffy a look that couldn't be described as anything but malicious. "I'm sorry, Buffy. This conversation is reserved for people who actually *have* a future."

Willow saw Buffy actually recoil, and Cordelia took the opportunity to stride off in victory.

For a long moment no one said anything as they watched her leave. Then Oz looked at Buffy. "An angry young woman."

"Oh, Buffy, she was just being Cordelia," Willow said sympathetically. She hated to see her best friend so wounded, no matter how much Buffy tried to mask it. "Only more so. Don't pay any attention to her."

"She's definitely got a chip going," Xander added.

Willow sent him a reproachful glance. "Maybe if you didn't *goad* her so much."

"I can't help it," Xander said. He seemed anything but apologetic. "It's my nature."

Willow frowned at him. "Maybe you need a better nature." She turned back to Buffy, but the Slayer wasn't listening. Instead, she was staring at the tabletop, lost in her own thoughts.

CHAPTER 2

She'd known he was going to be shocked, but Wesley was staring at her as though she'd suddenly grown three extra heads.

"I don't understand," he said.

They'd walked into the library together, and now Buffy stopped to face him. "Well, I don't think I can talk any slower, Wes. I want to leave."

"What?" he asked in confusion. "Now?"

"No, not now," Buffy said. She felt as if she was explaining physics to a five-year-old. Was it really that hard to comprehend? "After I graduate." Still, he just looked at her blankly. "College?" she reminded him loudly.

Wesley blinked. "But . . . you're a Slayer."

Buffy ground her teeth as she shrugged off her bag. "Yeah, I'm also a *person*. You can't just define me by my Slayerness—that's . . . something-ism." *Darn it, what's the word I was searching for?*

Giles came out of where he'd been listening from his office, the ever-present cup of tea in his hand. "Buffy, I know we've talked about you going away—"

"I got into Northwestern," she cut in happily.

The librarian's mouth dropped open, then he smiled, clearly pleased. "That's wonderful news. Good for you!"

"All right, everyone," Wesley said sharply. "Monsters, demons, world in peril?"

"I bet you they have all that stuff in Illinois," Buffy told him.

"You *cannot* leave Sunnydale." Wesley drew himself up and folded the first two fingers of each hand over his heart. "By the power invested in me by the Council," he said primly, "I forbid it."

Buffy rolled her eyes as Giles raised his cup with a disgusted glance at the other man. "Oh, yes—that should settle it."

Wesley waved a finger at Buffy and came toward them. "With Faith gone bad and the Mayor's Ascension coming up—"

"I know it's complicated," Buffy said, stopping his tirade. "I'm aware that my graduation may be, among other things, posthumous. But what if I . . . *stop* the Ascension? What if I capture Faith?"

Giles took off his glasses as he settled on a chair. "I very much hope you will, but—"

"If I do that," Buffy rushed on, "then all you guys have to do is keep the run-of-the-mill unholy forces at bay through midterms, and I'll be back here in time for homecoming, and every school break after that." She waited, but neither man said anything. "Can we at least think about it?"

Wesley at least tried to seem sympathetic. "Perhaps if circumstances were different—"

"I'll *make* them different," Buffy said.

Wesley frowned. "What?"

"I'm *tired* of waiting for Mayor McSleaze to make his move while we sit on our hands counting down to Ascension Day." She balled up her fist. "I say, let's take the fight to them."

"No," Wesley said firmly. *"No.* It's much too reckless. We're at a distinct disadvantage. We don't know anything about the Mayor's Ascension—"

"She's right," Giles said, standing. Wesley glared at him, but Giles kept right on going. "Time is running out—we need to take the offensive." He turned to Buffy. "What's your plan?"

She'd been grinning, but that did a fast fade. "I gotta have a plan?" She looked at him. "Really? I can't just be proactive with pep?"

Giles smiled in spite of himself. "No. You want to take the fight to them, I suggest the first step would be to find out exactly what they're up to."

"Oh," Buffy said. "I actually knew that. I thought you meant a more specific plan. You know, with maps and stuff." Giles and Wesley said nothing, and after a moment she squared her shoulders and picked up her bag. "Great. I'll find out what they're up to."

This was a part of the airport that was well off the main drag, far in the back and away from prying eyes. The people count was zero, and the only movement was the small, single-engine prop plane, itself relatively quiet, that taxied to a stop about seventy-five feet away from the Mayor's big black limousine. When the plane's engine shut down, the side door slid open, and a set of small metal steps swung down; in another moment someone exited, and Faith saw the boots first. Tacky light gray snakeskin with pointed toes—didn't these dopes ever look in a mirror?

The next thing she saw was the box—the Mayor's big prize. It was made of some kind of dark metal, very ornately engraved, with heavy latches on each side of the front. There was a carrying handle on the side, and from that swung one end of a locked pair of handcuffs. The other end of the cuffs was snapped around the wrist of the courier.

And wasn't he just your typical Male Unsavory Model? As if the boots, ugly jacket, and uglier-patterned shirt weren't enough, the guy had greasy hair slicked back into a tight ponytail, no chin, and a snake tattoo twisting around his neck and up the right side of his jaw all the way to his forehead. Nothing to make *him* stand out in your average, everyday crowd, no sir.

From her vantage point, Faith watched as the guy strode confidently up to the Mayor's driver, a timid and skinny vampire with about as much solid backbone as the serpent tattoo crawling across the delivery man's skin.

"He in the car?" Snake Face asked in a gravelly voice.

The driver opened the back door and motioned at the car's interior. "No. I'll take you to him."

Ticked, the courier reached out a booted foot and kicked the limo door closed. "The Mayor was supposed to be here in person," he growled. "With the money."

The driver shrugged nervously. "I—"

"Uh-huh," the courier said with a sneer. "Well, the price just went up. I don't *like* surprises."

His words made Faith grin evilly, and she let her finger squeeze, just so, on the object she was holding.

A high whistling sound cut through the air, and the courier jerked in front of the vampire driver. His eyes widened as he stared first forward, then down to his chest, as if he couldn't believe what he was seeing—

The point of an arrow protruding from the center of his rib cage.

He toppled forward and landed on his face, showing the rest of the arrow's shaft neatly embedded in his back. As the driver looked up and stared, Faith tucked her crossbow under one arm, stepped to the roof's edge of the low supply building on which she'd been perched a few yards away, and jumped down.

When she crossed the tarmac and joined the driver, he was still shocked. "You killed him!"

"What are you, the narrator?" she asked snidely. "Get the keys to the cuffs."

He looked at her anxiously, then bent and searched the dead man's pockets. The vamp shook his head. "Nothing."

Oh . . . too bad. She reached a hand inside her leather jacket and pulled the beautiful blade the Mayor had given her from the waistband of her pants.

The driver eyed it, then the box on the ground next to the newly deceased delivery man. "That won't cut through steel."

Faith held up the blade so that it gleamed in the nearby lights, then gave him a sweet, wicked smile. "No," she agreed. "But it'll cut through bone."

Dark, empty, and probably crawling with hungry danger—just your average after-dark evening in happy little Sunnydale. But Buffy's patient spying in the bushes by City Hall finally paid off when the Mayor's limousine pulled around to the front and stopped. She watched as the driver got out, then opened the back door; a second later, Faith exited, both arms wrapped around a large black box that was probably just the sort of thing to add to the excitement of something unknown like the Ascension. The dark-haired girl glanced around automatically, then quickly climbed the stairs to the government building and disappeared inside.

Buffy ducked down again as the driver got back into the limo, then followed when he drove the car around to the parking spaces at the back of the building. She waited until he cut the lights and ignition, and then, right before he would have opened the door, she smashed the driver's window with her fist and yanked him halfway through the opening.

Always opt for the element of surprise.

"So," she said, in her best Little-Miss-Friendly-and-Cheerful voice, "what's in the box?"

Faith burst through the doors of the Mayor's office with a flourish and set the black box down on the corner of his desk.

"Hey-ho, there it is!" the Mayor said happily. He stood, then reached into his coat pocket and pulled out an envelope. "Uh—where's the courier? I was supposed to pay him . . ."

"Huh." Faith said nonchalantly. "I . . . made him an offer he couldn't survive." She grinned, took the envelope from his hand, and flipped it open to peer at the cash inside.

Mayor Wilkins looked surprised, but only for a moment. "You are one *heck* of a girl!" He gave a delighted laugh. "Jeez, the initiative, the skill—"

"Go on, go on," Faith said, basking.

"I will," he told her as she settled on the chair across from his desk. "I—hey, hey, hey!"

Faith froze, taken aback, then realized he was flipping because she'd put her booted feet on his desk. *Oops.*

Relaxing again when she dropped them to the floor, the Mayor continued, "If Buffy Summers walked in here and said she wanted to switch to our side, I'd say, 'No thanks, sister! I've got all the Slayer one man could ever need!' "

Great, Faith thought. *It always comes back to Buffy.* Aloud she only sighed.

Wilkins looked at her quizzically. "What?"

Why bother? "Nothing," she said.

Realization etched his features. "Oh . . . it's because I used the B-word. Don't tell me you're still sore about that whole Angel-Buffy thing?"

"No, I'm over it." Faith stood and paced around the room. "She can have him."

"You better believe she can," Mayor Wilkins said merrily. "She deserves that poor excuse for a creature of the night."

He turned away and fiddled with something on his credenza. Only half listening, Faith wandered over and undid the two latches on the front of the Mayor's box, then started to lift the lid. He swung back around. "You, on the other hand—"

Faith had never thought the old man could move as fast as he did when he leaped out of his chair and slammed the box shut again. The anxious expression on his face was immediately replaced by a plastered-on, vaguely sickly smile.

"Don't do that."

CHAPTER 3

"The Box of Gavrock," Willow heard Buffy tell Xander and Wesley as they were leaning over and looking at a mound of research books on the table. "It houses some great demonic energy or something which His Honor needs to chow down on come A-Day."

Willow and Giles joined them at the library table, unrolling a detailed floor plan while Buffy and Xander weighed down the corners with books.

"What's that?" asked Wesley.

Giles looked at Buffy. "Maps and stuff."

"Plans for City Hall," Willow offered. "They were in the water and power mainframe."

"The box is being kept under guard in a conference room on the top floor." Buffy scanned the floor plan until she found what she wanted and pointed. "There. Unfortunately, that's all I could get out of my informant before his aggressive tendencies forced me to introduce him to Mr. Pointy."

Wesley nodded sagely. "Well, now," he said. "Here's what I think we should do—"

"I figure we can enter through the skylight," Buffy interrupted. "I'll take Angel with me."

"Agreed," Giles said.

Xander tapped a spot on the right side of the floor plan. "There's a fire ladder on the east side of the building here."

"Yes, fine," Wesley said. "But you'll still need to consider whether—"

"It won't be enough simply to gain possession of the box," Giles noted. He reached under the plans and withdrew one of the leather-bound books, quickly opening it and flipping to the page he needed.

"Right," Willow added. "We have to destroy it. Not just physically but ritually." She smiled, pleased. "With some down-and-dirty black magic."

Wesley straightened. "Hang on. We don't know what such a ritual would require—"

"I think the Breath of the Entropics is standard for this sort of thing," Giles said without missing a beat. "Fairly simple recipe."

The librarian offered the book to Xander. "I know," Xander said. "I'm ingredient-getting guy." He turned to leave.

"All right, *stop!*" Wesley said loudly, and held up his hand. "I demand everyone stop this *instant!*"

Willow and the others froze.

"*I* am in charge here," Wesley announced stiffly. "And I say this is all moving much too fast. We need time to fully analyze the situation and devise a proper and effective strategic . . . stratagem."

Buffy moved away from Willow's side, going nose-to-nose with her so-called Watcher. "Wes, hop on the train or get off the tracks."

"The Mayor will most assuredly have supernatural safeguards protecting the box," Wesley protested. When no one said anything, he looked smugly down his nose at them. "Oh, we all *forgot* about that, did we?"

Buffy glanced in Willow's direction. "Looks like a job for Wiccan Girl. What do you say, Will? Big-time danger."

Willow grinned from ear to ear. "I eat danger for breakfast."

Xander tilted his head. "But oddly enough, she panics in the face of breakfast foods."

Buffy ignored him. "Let's get to work."

Willow and Giles handed the now-rumpled floor plans to Wesley and hurried out with the others.

Ingredient Man to the rescue! Xander thought as he hustled along on his errands. Only one more thing to get—

He halted in front of the picture window of an exclusive little dress shop downtown. Was that . . . could it be . . . Cordelia?

He should keep going. After all, he had errands to do, important things to procure. He really didn't have time to exchange petty insults with his viper-tongued former girl-friend—

Xander smiled. Sure he did.

When he pushed through the front door, Cordy was admiring a slinky, sparkling black dress. As she was replacing the hanger on the rack, Xander spoke. "I have a theory."

Cordelia turned and saw him, and for a moment she actually looked a bit fearful. Obviously a mistake—he couldn't imagine why he would ever make her nervous— so he just plunged on. "Your snide remarks earlier? I'm guessing grapes a little on the sour side." Her eyes narrowed—there was the Cordelia he knew and loved—but she said nothing. "Didn't get into any schools, did you?" Xander continued. "Grades were there, but ooooh, if it weren't for that pesky interview." He nodded, certain he was on the mark. "Ten minutes with you, and the admissions department decided they'd already reached their mean-spirited, superficial princess quota."

But Cordelia only lifted her chin. "And once again the gold medal in the Being Wrong Event goes to Xander 'I'm As Stupid As I Look' Harris," she snapped. She spun and retrieved a packet of letters from where her purse lay on a chair, then read them off one by one as she handed them to him. "Read 'em and weep, creep. U.S.C., Colorado State, Duke, and . . . Columbia."

"Wow," Xander said, momentarily humbled. "These are . . . great colleges. I'm guessing they must have seen a different side of your father's money."

Gotcha, Xander thought as she hesitated. It was rare, indeed, to see Cordelia without a comeback, but this time she only snatched her envelopes out of his hand and shoved them back into her purse. "Go away," she hissed.

"Sure," he said with an uppity smile. "If you'll excuse me, I have to get back to helping to save lives." He waved a hand at the store. "Carry on—I know that you have some important accessorizing to do."

Xander spun on his heel and left. There'd been an expression on her face at his parting shot he couldn't understand—almost like hurt, but he had important stuff to do, and he couldn't let himself think about that.

Wesley pulled the unmarked black van into the alley behind City Hall, and Willow climbed out after Buffy and Angel, who had a full rig of cable and pulleys draped over one arm. She and the others stopped at the passenger window to see if Giles had any final words of instruction.

But there wasn't much to say. Giles eyed them all over the thermos he always seemed to carry with him on such outings. "Now remember," he told the three of them, "if anything should go awry, Wesley and I will create a diversion."

Wesley leaned forward so he could be seen. "Let's synchronize our watches," he said briskly. "I have twenty-one for—" He stopped when they all held up watchless wrists. "Yes," he said in contempt. "Typical."

Willow grinned mischievously. "Maybe we can just count one-one-thousand, two-one-thousand—"

"Be careful," Giles said before she could get any farther. "All of you."

She and Buffy nodded, and the three of them headed toward the back of City Hall. As Angel pulled down the fire escape ladder and gave her a boost onto it, Willow almost laughed when she heard Giles say, faintly, to Wesley, "Tea?"

Just another night on the town in Sunnydale.

Oz looked up as Xander hurried into the library with a bag in his hands. "You got the goods?" he asked as he carefully positioned the large pot they were going to use as a cauldron for the spell to destroy the Box of Gavrock.

"Yeah," the dark-haired teen replied. He rummaged through the bag and began pulling out plastic-wrapped pouches. "Essence of toad. Twice-blessed sage . . ." He hesitated as he held up the greenish powder. "Or maybe that's the toad."

Oz studied him. "Well, we'd better be sure." He took the pouch carefully. "Destroying this box is supposed to be a pretty delicate operation."

For a second, Xander looked frustrated. "Then they shouldn't have left it in the hands of the lay people."

Oz motioned Xander to follow him to the library table. "Will set it out for us pretty well."

"Wow, she even drew helpful diagrams," Xander agreed as he studied the piece of pink paper Oz offered. "There's the pedestal."

"Uh-huh." Oz pointed. "And us. See, there's you, there's me."

Xander peered at the drawing. "How can you tell which is which? I mean, they both look kind of stick-fig-urey to me."

"This one's me—see the little guitar?"

Xander nodded. "Gotcha."

Oz smiled a little as he eyed the tiny figures. "Yeah. Nobody like my Will."

"No, sir," Xander agreed. "There is not."

Without needing to say anything, Xander headed to the table, and Oz went for the waiting cauldron to drop in the first of the ingredients.

"Okay," Oz said. "Toad me."

They could see the Box of Gavrock through one of the murky panes in the skylight.

There it was, sitting in the middle of the conference room table right below them. It looked just like a . . . box. Who would have thought it had some nasty little spell protecting it, some innocuous-seeming thing that would probably burn your hand right off your body if you touched it?

Ah, but Willow was fighting the Good Fight, and she would handle that, by cracky.

Angel quietly lifted open the skylight while Willow opened the book she'd gotten from Giles. At her side, Buffy waited for her signal, then handed over a small jar of fine blue powder. Willow carefully sprinkled it through the opening, watching as it settled lightly over the box, not touching the box's surface but floating above it by a good three inches.

She said the spell first in Latin—*"Sis modo dissolutum exposco, validum scutum! Diutius nec defend a manibus ocroam, intende!"*—then in English, just to be sure—"Be now dissolved, I demand, o powerful shield; no longer defend the box from our hands. Hear us!"

The last word had barely left her lips when the layer of dull powder suddenly sparkled wildly, then fell onto the box's top with a small *poof* as the protective shield vanished.

Willow grinned, extremely pleased with herself. "Oh, yeah," she said. "I'm bad."

"Four stars, Will," Buffy said in approval. Her friend's expression turned serious. "Now get gone."

"I'm gone," Willow said agreeably, and hurried back to the fire escape ladder. As she climbed over the edge of the roof and started down, she saw Angel buckling Buffy into a rapelling harness and sent up a silent prayer to the Powers That Be that they would both be all right.

Okay, Buffy thought as Angel slowly lowered her into the room. *I can do without the* Mission Impossible *music in my head.*

Still, there it was, brought about by some offhanded comment up on the roof as she'd climbed into the harness—poor Angel probably had it going through his mind as well. Lower, and lower . . .

Just before her feet could touch the table she tilted her body forward and grabbed hold of the handles on each side of the box. *Here goes nothing.*

She lifted it.

And the alarm went off.

Was there ever a doubt?

"Got it!" Buffy yelled over her shoulder. Angel obliged by reversing directions on the pulley; she went up about three inches, then stopped.

Okay, this was quickly getting to be un-fun. "Angel?"

"It's jammed," she heard her boyfriend say between his teeth. The next thing she heard was running footsteps, louder and louder as they approached the conference room doors. Were they locked? One could only hope.

"Like very much to come up now, please," she called. Nothing happened; hanging in the air made her feel like a human marshmallow on a rope, just dangling there for the vampire takers. Beyond the closed doors, she heard the unmistakable sound of keys jangling, then the lock clicked. *"Angel!"*

"I *know!*" he said frantically.

The doors to the conference room burst open, and two guards, both vampires, rushed in. They skidded to a stop, momentarily stunned by the sight of the Slayer dangling there in the air.

She gave them a sickly smile but held on to the box. "Don't suppose you'd want to help me get down?"

They snarled in response.

"Didn't think so."

They lunged, but Angel was there, dropping onto the table in time to kick the first one in the head and send him sprawling. Buffy tossed him the box, then pivoted her body until she was upright so she could unhook herself from the harness. In front of her Angel ducked a punch, then hit his attacker with the box before dropping it on the creature's instep with a solid *crunch*. As Buffy sent the other sprawling with a good kick, Angel knocked the second bloodsucker across the room. It seemed as if punches and kicks were everywhere, and they were taking as good as they got—at one point one of the vampires threw a chair at Angel, who caught it instead and brought it down on the thing's head. Buffy and Angel passed the box back and forth between swings, determined to keep it out of the wrong hands; as she hammered one vampire into the back wall, then took him down with a triple flip, Angel threw the other one clear over the conference room table. Finally, with the box firmly under Angel's arm, she and Angel paired off and turned the conference room table over and onto the fallen bloodsuckers, pinning them to the floor long enough to get the heck out of Dodge—or at least the Mayor's office.

It didn't take long for the guards to find their footing and come after them. Buffy and Angel were maybe two turns ahead of their pursuers when they flew through the front doors of City Hall and into the night air. A quick left-right look, then they dove into the bushes on their right, hoping that Giles and Wesley were paying attention rather than arguing about something scintillating such as the Watchers Council retreats.

And indeed the two older men were right on the ball. As the vampires surged onto the front steps, they were met with the sight of the black van peeling away from the curb as though it had stopped to pick up the humans they were chasing. The vamps ran after it, uselessly, disappearing down the block as Giles and Wesley laughed out the window like a couple of wild teenagers.

Relieved, Buffy and Angel watched them go, then melted into the darkness with the Box of Gavrock.

"Well, this is *very* unfortunate." Mayor Wilkins, outwardly calm, waved a hand at what was left of his formerly beautiful conference room. Everything in sight seemed to be shattered—vase, lamps, chairs, the maple conference room table, even the skylight had come down to join the chaos. "I just had this conference room redecorated, for Pete's sake," he complained. "At taxpayers' expense."

He bent and righted one of the chairs, then leaned on it. "And, oh yeah—*they've got my BOX!*"

"Yeah, they do," came Faith's cheerful voice. About to throw the chair, Wilkins swiveled as she came into the room, practically skipping with happiness. "But lookee what *we* got!"

The Mayor's scowl melted into a pleased smile as his dark-haired Slayer yanked someone forward. *Is it . . . can it be . . .*

Ah, yes. Willow. The little redhead with the annoyingly nimble computer skills.

He felt his pleasant smile turn downright evil.

CHAPTER 4

"**H**ow did you guys—how did this *happen?*" Buffy was so freaked—well, they *all* were—that she was nearly screaming.

"We thought she stayed with you," Giles said. Neither he nor Wesley could look at her. Xander was in shock, actually speechless, and Oz was like a stone statue.

"They must have grabbed her when she hit the ground," Angel said. "Buffy, I'm sorry—"

Her hand cut through the air, silencing him. "Look, it's nobody's fault, okay? We just need to focus and *deal.*" She glanced at Oz and saw he hadn't moved; he was just standing there, silent and vaguely dangerous. "Oz, I *swear* I won't let them hurt her."

"We go back," Xander said suddenly. "Full-on assault."

Giles shook his head. "They'll kill her."

"We're assuming they haven't already." Wesley glanced at Buffy.

"No, no." Buffy paced back and forth, trying to think. "They know what she means to us. She's too valuable, and as long as we still have . . ." She turned her gaze to the library table and what was on it. "The . . . box." Her expression hardened. "We trade."

"We can't," Wesley said immediately.

Buffy ignored him and faced Giles. "No, it's the safest plan, it's the *only* way. Right?"

"It might well be—" Giles began.

Wesley scowled at him as Buffy began organizing her thoughts aloud. "We call the Mayor," she said, "and arrange a meeting."

"The box must be destroyed," Wesley interrupted sharply.

"I need a volunteer to hit Wesley," Xander put it.

The younger Watcher looked to Giles for support. "Giles, you know I'm right about this."

Buffy's expression was ominous. "Wes, you want to duck and cover at this point?"

"Damn it, you listen to me!" Wesley's shouted words were enough to make them all freeze in place.

"This box," the dark-haired man told them, "is the key to the Mayor's Ascension. *Thousands* of lives depend upon our getting rid of it." His voice softened. "Now, I want to help Willow as much as the rest of you, but we will find another way."

"There *is* no other way," Buffy said through clenched teeth.

Wesley glared at her. *"You're* the one who said take the fight to the Mayor, and you were right. This is the town's best hope of survival." He paused, searching. "It's your best chance to get out!"

Buffy's eyes widened. "You think I *care* about that?" She took a step toward him. "Are you made of human parts?"

"All right," Giles broke in. "Let's deal with this rationally—"

"I can't believe you're taking his side!" Buffy shouted.

"No one said I was taking his side," Giles said hotly.

Angel tried to break in over the escalating volume. "None of this is helping—"

Xander had to add his three cents. "I'm still for the 'let's hit Wesley' movement, if anyone cares—"

"Listen to you people!" Wesley's pinched voice rose over them all. "You'd sacrifice thousands of lives—your families, your friends? It can all end right here! We have the means to destroy this box—"

Buffy saw Oz go for it, but he was faster than she'd ever seen him except in werewolf mode. Before the Watcher could finish his sentence—

CRASH!

—and those "means," the cauldron with the Breath of the Entropics spell ready and waiting, went spinning off its pedestal and hit the floor, shattering into a thousand pieces.

All the shouting stopped as Oz calmly turned and faced Buffy. She looked at him, then at the librarian, ignoring the rigid expression on Wesley's face.

"Giles," she said. "Make the phone call."

Okay, this was not where Willow had been planning on spending her evening.

Small room, nearly empty except for a banged-up old desk, a dingy light, and a bunch of boring file boxes—obviously some kind of storage space for mostly forgotten stuff. If only she could count on her captors forgetting *her* until she figured a way to get out of this mess. Not very likely.

She tried the window, but it was bolted shut, and the glass was shot through with that safety wire stuff—even if she broke it, she'd just be facing metal. The boxes were filled with nothing but old papers, but there had to be *something* useful in here—how about in the desk? Willow pulled out the drawers, but there wasn't much to see, and when she pulled too hard on the last one, it came clear out of the desk and crashed to the floor. Great; nothing like drawing attention to herself, and all she got for her troubles was the standard desk-type contents—a few old paper clips, some rubber bands, a pencil. She started to reach down and go through the stuff, then heard the door being unlocked.

Uh-oh.

The guard who pushed open the door had probably been a nice enough looking guy when he was human; as a vampire, he was pretty repulsive. "What are you doing?" he demanded.

"Oh," Willow said, trying to sound innocent. "Ummm, I'm . . . looking for a sucking candy. My mouth gets dry when I'm nervous, or held prisoner against my will . . ." She backed away from him, and he licked his lips and stepped toward her. ". . . and suddenly I'm thinking that *sucking* isn't a good word to use around vampires."

He didn't respond, just drifted toward her, his beady yellow gaze fixed firmly in the area of her neck.

She was terrified, but that wasn't going to help her now. "Hey," she said sharply, trying to snap him out of his hunger-induced trance, "did you get permission to eat the hostage? I don't think so." Her back was almost against the wall now, with that uselessly wired window on her right. "You're going to be in some trouble here when the Mayor—"

She forgot what she was saying when he actually reached out and grabbed her. *"No!"*

"Just a little taste," he hissed at her. He leaned forward, and she scrunched her shoulders up tight, trying to make her neck as small and unavailable as possible. His mouth opened, smelling cold, stinky, and definitely undead. She concentrated—

thinking

thinking

thinking

—then opened her eyes and stared right into his face. Behind him, the pencil from the desk drawer floated upward and spun lazily in the air, repositioning itself just so . . .

. . . and slammed point first into the center of his back. The vamp guy gawked at her, then dustized.

Freed of his grasp, Willow stumbled forward, smiling even so. But there was no time for self-pats-on-the-back—she had to get out of here, and fast. Scurrying to the door, she checked in both directions, then crept down the deserted hallway. There were offices on both sides, all handily labeled with name plates, but darn it, she just couldn't find the one that read "Escape." She tried one big door that looked as if it led out and found it was locked; she took a few more steps, then ducked into a doorway when she heard Faith's nastily familiar voice.

"They're not going to be brain-damaged enough to come back here tonight."

Peering out ever so carefully, Willow saw Faith and the Mayor come out of an office above which hung a fancier-than-most name plate that read "Mayor Richard Wilkins III." They walked chummily side by side, away from her hiding place.

"Ever have a dog?" the Mayor asked Faith.

"What?"

"I did." To Willow's ears, his voice sounded absurdly like a storyteller in front of an audience. "I did—Rusty. Irish setter, swell little pooch. A dog's friendship is stronger than reason, stronger than its own sense of self-preservation."

They turned the corner as Willow listened to his tale, gritting her teeth at what she heard. "Buffy's like a dog," Wilkins told Faith. His voice faded in Willow's ears as he and Faith made their way out. "And, hey—before you can say 'Jack Robinson,' you'll get to see me kill her like one."

Not likely, thought Willow as she peeked out of her doorway to make sure they hadn't changed their minds and come back. She really ought to hunt for the way out, maybe even see if that's where Faith and Wilkins had been headed, but . . .

The Mayor's office beckoned.

Heart pounding, Willow slipped through the partially opened doors and into His Honor's inner sanctum. She closed the doors behind her and glanced around. It didn't look like much—fancy desk and leather chairs, fancier couch for visitors and lots of stuffy, governmental-looking paintings with gilded frames on the walls. Dim lighting—maybe that meant he'd gone home for the night, leaving her in the care of his guard . . . and what a dumb choice *that* had been. Nothing in sight but ordinary, dull, everyday Mayor stuff, and maybe she ought to just get the heck out of here while she cou—

Hold it a second.

What was that on the opposite wall?

Some kind of built-in wooden cabinet, probably nothing but city code books or something. Still, just to make sure, Willow crossed the room and cautiously opened it.

"Whoa," she said in a low voice.

It was full of dark mojo stuff—skulls, charms of every shape and size, shrunken heads, and dark little boxes containing who knew what kinds of evil. Bones abounded— big ones from arms to little ones still held together by wire . . . or something else . . . to maintain their hand shapes; there were iron goblets and hourglasses and little unidentifiable pincer-looking thingies that were probably implements of torture she didn't want to learn about. Then, when Willow knelt to get a better look at the stuff along the mostly empty lower shelf, she saw a tiny lever on the underside of the upper one. Without hesitating, she pushed it.

Doors in the wall at the back of the shelf slid open, and Willow found herself looking at—

"The Books of Ascension," she whispered.

A furtive peek over her shoulder to make sure the office doors were still shut, and she reached for the first book. She really needed to get the heck out of there, but she'd just glance through it quickly and see if there was anything useful . . .

"Check out the bookworm."

Oops.

Where had the time gone . . . shoot, how *much* of it had gone? And with that her common sense—she'd lost it so thoroughly that she had all five books spread on the floor and open to various chapters and passages, had been scanning page after page and trying to absorb as much of it as she could. Spells, diagrams, prayers, it was all here. Along with—

"Faith!"

The dark-haired Slayer shook her head in amazement and knelt next to where Willow had made herself a comfortable nest among the heavy volumes. "Anybody with brains, anybody who *knew* what was going to happen to her, would be trying to claw her way out of this place. But you . . ." Faith's mouth twisted. "You just can't stop Nancy Drewing, can you?" She reached out and slammed shut the book on Willow's lap, narrowly missing Willow's fingers. "I guess now you know too much. And that kind of just naturally leads to killing."

Faith started to lean toward her, and Willow decided now would be a good time to get back on her feet. "Faith," she stammered as she scrambled up. "I . . . want to talk to you."

The other girl put on an expression of exaggerated patience. "Oh, yeah—please." She sneered. "Give me the speech again: 'Faith, we're still your friends, we can help you, it's not too late.' "

But Willow only looked at her. "Oh, it's way too late." Faith's grin faded to disbelief. "It didn't have to be this way," Willow continued, "but you made your choice. I know you've had a tough life. I know that some people think you've had a lot of bad breaks." Faith's eyes softened, but Willow wasn't here to make friends—having a knife at her throat earlier had pretty much nixed any chance of that, no matter what excuses Buffy kept trying to make for her *co*-Slayer. "Well, boo-hoo," Willow snapped. "Poor you—you had a *lot* more in your life than some people. I mean, you had friends like Buffy. Now you've got no one—and you were a Slayer! Now you're nothing." Willow stared at her. "You're just a big, selfish, worthless . . . waste."

For a moment, Faith said nothing. Then her fist flashed out and connected with Willow's jaw, hard. She flew backward and went down, stars swirling in her head. The only good thing about it was that Faith had hit her so hard her face had actually gone a little numb—though later she would probably feel this big-time. If she *had* a later.

"You hurt me, I hurt you," Faith said almost cheerfully. "I'm just a little more efficient.

Willow looked at her dully as she wobbled back to her

feet. "Awww, and here I just thought you didn't have a comeback."

Faith slapped her hands against Willow's collarbone, pushing her backward. "You're begging for some deep pain."

"I'm not afraid of you." A lie, and the Slayer could probably tell that by the way Willow's breath was starting to come in short gasps.

Faith smiled evilly and reached inside her leather jacket. When she pulled her hand out, it came complete with a long, elaborately curved knife. "Let's see what we can do about that," she whispered.

Terrified, Willow still lifted her chin and faced the other girl. She would *not* give her the satisfaction of backing down or begging. Faith would have to—

"Girls?"

Over Faith's shoulder, Willow saw the Mayor standing in the doorway, his hands casually in his pockets. "I hope I don't have to separate you two," he said. "Faith, you can play with your new toy later. Something's come up."

Still furious, Faith didn't take her gaze from Willow's. She still held the knife between them, its edge only a breath from Willow's cheek.

"Faith," Wilkins said sharply. She glanced at him reluctantly. "You know I don't like repeating myself."

Faith glared at Willow a final time, then lowered the knife. "I've got someone," she said to Willow in a low voice. "I've got *him*."

Willow inhaled as Faith walked over and sat on the edge of the Mayor's desk. Wilkins plopped onto his chair, then leaned forward and rested his chin on his palm, grinning happily as he looked over at Willow.

"I just received one *heck* of an interesting phone call."

CHAPTER 5

"The whole place is locked down," Buffy heard Oz say. "Except for the front."

She'd sent him and Xander to check out all the doors and windows in the cafeteria to make sure, since this was where they'd agreed to meet Mayor Wilkins and trade the Box of Gavrock for Willow. Giles, holding tight to a baseball bat, peered out one of the windows while Wesley stood to the side. The young Watcher wasn't pleased, but then she really didn't give a rat's butt. In fact, he ought to be glad they had the box to trade—Buffy gladly would have offered him instead.

Xander shuddered and eyed the corners of the big room. "Gives me that comforting 'trapped' feeling."

"One way out means one way in," Buffy said firmly. "I want to see them coming."

The lights went out.

Xander jerked and automatically looked at the now-darkened fluorescents. "I guess they're shy."

Standing next to Buffy, Angel smiled and blinked slowly, like a cat waiting for the kill. "I can see all right." He watched as the others armed themselves, then stood.

Ready and waiting.

Ten steps ahead of her, the Mayor's two vampire henchmen shoved open the doors of the cafeteria.

Mayor Wilkins strode through as though he were a king, with Faith and Willow right behind him. Willow's entrance, unfortunately, was less than spectacular—having a line of sharp, cold steel pressing against her throat kind of took the pizzazz out of her appearance. Buffy and the others moved to meet the Mayor, then everybody stopped all at once—funny, but even from Willow's scrunched-up spot beneath Faith's less-than-gentle forearm, she thought they all looked like mirroring pieces on a chessboard. Who would make the first move?

Mayor Wilkins stepped forward at the same time as Buffy did.

For a moment, no one said anything. Then, outlandishly, the Mayor actually laughed. "Well, this is exciting, isn't it?" He grinned, but there was nothing pleasant about it. "Clandestine meetings by dark of night, exchange of prisoners—I just feel like we should all be wearing trench coats."

"Let her go," Buffy said in a hard voice.

"No," Mayor Wilkins said just as coldly. "Not until the box is in my hands." He studied her for a moment. "So you're the little girl who's been causing me all this trouble." He looked over at Angel. "She's pretty, Angel. Little skinny . . . I still don't understand why it couldn't work out with you and my Faith." His eyes glittered oddly in the dimness. "Guess you just have strange taste in women."

Angel didn't hesitate. "Yeah, well, what can I say? I like 'em sane."

Nice comeback, Willow decided, even worth it when Faith got ticked and tightened her steel-enhanced stranglehold. She could have just pinched herself for the little whimper that escaped, though.

"Angel," she heard Oz warn quietly.

"Well," the Mayor said in a disgustingly buddy-buddy voice, "I wish you kids the best, I really do. But if you don't mind a bit of fatherly advice, I . . . well, just don't see much of a future for you two." He looked from Buffy to Angel. "I don't sense a lasting relationship, and not just because I plan to kill both of you. But you have a bumpy road ahead."

If daggers could have come out of Buffy's eyes, Willow knew the Mayor's face would've looked like a stiletto-filled bull's eye. "I don't think we need to talk about this."

Mayor Wilkins shrugged. "You kids . . . you know, you don't like to think about the future, don't like to make plans." He glanced over his shoulder at where Faith held on to Willow, and Willow *really* didn't like the expression on his face. His next words just confirmed her intuition. "Unless you want Faith to gut your friend like a sea bass, you'll show a little respect for your elders."

"You're not my elder," Angel said flatly. "I've got a lot of years on you."

The older man's eyebrows rose. "Yeah, and that's just *one* of the things you're going to have to deal with." He gestured at Buffy, then actually looked sad. "You're immortal, she's not. It's not easy. I married my Edna Mae in aught three, and I was with her right until the end. Not a pretty picture—wrinkled and senile and cursing me for my youth." He shook his head. "It wasn't our happiest time."

Buffy and Angel just stared at him, not speaking, but Willow could see that although they were steely-eyed on the surface, the Mayor had indeed hit a nerve. He took a couple of unhurried steps forward, talking as though he were thinking out loud. "And let's forget the fact that any moment of true happiness will turn you evil. What kind of a life can you offer her? I don't see a lot of Sunday picnics in the offing." He ran a finger thoughtfully along one of the lunch tables. "I see skulking in the shadows, hiding from the sun . . . she's a blossoming girl, and you want to keep her from the life she should have until it's passed her by?" He was in front of Angel now, face to face with the vampire. "By God, I think that's a little selfish—is that what you came back from Hell for? Is *that* your greater purpose?"

No one moved, and Willow could see that the Mayor had cut Buffy and Angel to the core—his success was written on the face of everyone in the room. Even Giles looked pained, and while she couldn't see Faith, Willow didn't doubt for a moment that her expression was one of pure victory.

The Mayor shot Angel a final, disgusted glance, then turned and walked back to his original spot. "Make the trade."

Faith pushed Willow forward, and Angel stepped up to her, the Box of Gavrok ready. Willow stumbled as Faith let her go, put away her blade, and pulled the box from Angel's hands. For a moment they all stood there, faintly surprised.

"Well," the Mayor said gleefully. "That went as smoothly as could be—"

Crash!

Everyone in the room whirled to face the side door as it slammed open and Principal Snyder stomped into the room, followed by two security guards. One of the guards reached back and locked the doors behind them, then Willow saw a third guard come through the cafeteria's front doors and lock those, too. From the corner of her eye, she saw Wilkins step ever so quietly back into the shadows.

"Nobody moves," Snyder barked as he stopped next to Buffy. "I *knew* you kids were up to something!"

"Snyder, get *out* of here," Buffy said.

The little man's mouth turned down. "You're not giving orders, young lady." He reached over and yanked the box out of Faith's grip. Not sure what to do, the dark-haired Slayer looked over at the Mayor, then back at the principal.

"I suppose you're going to tell me I won't find drugs in this box," Snyder said scornfully. He turned and handed the Box of Gavrok to one of the guards. Facing his back, Faith hardened her expression and pulled the knife out of her waistband.

"Wait!" Buffy protested.

Mayor Wilkins stepped from the shadows. "Principal Snyder, I think we have a problem."

Snyder turned at the sound of the Mayor's voice and found his nose nearly touching the pointed end of Faith's knife as she gazed at him. His eyes bulged. "Mr. Mayor," he stuttered. "I—I had no idea you were—" Still focused on the gleaming steel an inch away, he backed up slowly. "I'm terribly sorry."

"It's I who should apologize," the Mayor said smoothly. "I mean, coming here at night—what must you be thinking?"

Willow turned her head and saw the guard by the box peering at it curiously. Surely he wouldn't—

"See," Mayor Wilkins continued, "I just need to—" He

broke off and looked past Snyder. "Uh—no! *Don't do that!*"

Too late.

Willow and everyone else in the cafeteria jumped when something black, leathery, and incredibly *fast* shot from the opened box and attached itself to the too-curious guard's face.

He screamed in pain—

—and collapsed.

CHAPTER 6

The guard fell, writhing on the floor as he tried to pull off the thing on his face. No good—before anyone could even *think* to react, the man's movements stopped, and the suspiciously spiderlike creature scuttled away into the darkness at floor level.

Taking most of the guard's face with it.

One of the other security guards retched behind his hand while Wesley said in a choked voice, "Oh . . . God."

Xander jerked, trying to see anything and everything on the floor. "Where'd it go?" he demanded.

"Get that door open!" Snyder ordered the two remaining security guards.

"No!" shouted Giles. "We can't let that thing out of here!" The guard with the keys ignored him and fumbled to open the door, succeeding only in dropping them.

"I still want to know where it went," Xander said. He

turned in a circle, the blackboard pointer he'd chosen as a weapon at the ready.

Willow saw Buffy hold up a finger. "Listen," the Slayer whispered. She stared intently at the ceiling, and the others followed her gaze . . . but they could see nothing. Even the Mayor looked up—

—and the spider creature dropped onto his face.

"Boss!" Faith yelled, and ran to him as he lurched backward. Without pausing, Faith grabbed the creature's back and ripped it off the Mayor, then threw the thing sideways. It rolled, then found its footing and scampered into the shadows by Wesley and Giles. Each man immediately climbed atop a chair and a table to keep their distance, while the Mayor, his face perforated in nearly a dozen places where the spider had started consuming it, sat up groggily. In trying to keep tabs on the escaped creature, Willow saw Snyder staring at the Mayor as His Honor's face reformed . . . and healed. To say the principal looked shocked would have been an understatement, then Willow realized that, of course, Snyder would have no clue about the Mayor's invulnerability . . . or anything else that was going on.

Wait—had she seen something else, another spider thingy—crawl out of the box? Willow couldn't be sure, but as the Mayor shook off the effects of his attack, he, too, focused on the container. "I wouldn't leave that open," he said matter-of-factly.

Buffy whirled just as another of the little beasts was getting a hold on the edge. She dove forward and hit the lid, slamming it shut and severing two of the spider's legs. Then its missing cousin dropped onto her back. Without thinking, she threw herself backward and down, crushing it.

Was that all of them—could they be sure? Angel pulled Buffy up and kicked the dead carcass aside as everybody peered around the room. Then Willow saw Faith focus on Wesley, grimace, and pull out her knife.

Wesley saw her, too, just as she drew back. *"No!"* he howled, and threw up his hands.

Cold steel, end over end, sailed past his shoulder and hit the last of the spider beasts dead center on the wall behind him.

The door clattered as the guard finally got it unlocked and bolted, followed quickly by the other guard and the Mayor's two vampires. Nobody else said anything for a long moment. Finally, Oz looked over at the Mayor. "Is that all of them?"

Wilkins picked up the box tenderly, then turned to face Buffy. "Not really. There's about fifty . . . *billion* of these happy little critters in here. Would you like to see?"

Buffy scowled and took a step toward him, then halted when he lifted the lid, just a bit. "Raise your hand if you're invulnerable," he said softly. He closed it again. "Faith, let's go."

The dark-haired Slayer hesitated, then Willow saw her look over to where her knife was still embedded in the wall through the back of the dead creature. Between her and her weapon stood so many of the people she despised—Willow, Giles, Wesley, Angel. Faith wanted her weapon badly, Willow knew, but her obedience to Wilkins would have to come first.

"Faith!" the Mayor commanded.

Faith glanced at the knife a final time, then followed him out and into the darkness.

Willow inhaled and saw the others also trying to pull it together. Buffy looked over at the principal, who had picked up a chair to use as a shield and now stood as though frozen. "Snyder, you alive in there?"

He came back with a snap. "You," he hissed at her, then

his gaze swept the rest of them. "All of you . . . why can't you be dealing drugs like *normal* people?" Still clutching his chair, he spun and stalked out of the cafeteria.

As Oz held her tightly, Willow saw Buffy shrug, then cross to the wall and pull out Faith's knife, letting the spider's corpse fall to the floor.

"Well," Wesley said bitterly, "that went swimmingly."

But Buffy only looked at the knife, then at Willow. A small smile played across her lips as their eyes met. "We did all right."

With Oz's arm comfortably across her shoulders, Willow smiled back.

Sitting on the library table with her legs tucked under her, Willow knew her words were coming almost too fast to understand as she told her best friend the story of her imprisonment ordeal. "So Faith is like, 'I'm gonna beat you up,' and I'm all, 'I'm not afraid of you,' and then she had the knife, which was less fun, but oh—and then I told her, 'You made your choice, Buffy was your friend—' "

"Yes," Giles interrupted. "That's fascinating—but let's get back to the point." His expression was a study in impatience. "You actually had your hands on the Books of Ascension?"

Willow nodded. "Volumes one through five."

The librarian's hands fluttered in the air. "Is there anything you can remember that can be of use to us? Anything at all?" He stared at her hopefully.

Willow made a "probably not" face. "Well, I was in a hurry. And . . . and what I did read was kind of involved. If you ask me? Way overwritten."

Giles looked utterly crushed. "Oh."

"Actually," Willow amended. "There *were* a few pages that were kind of interesting, but I didn't have a chance to read them fully." She gave it a beat, then pulled a wad of folded-up paper—about ten pages' worth—out of her pocket and offered them to him. "See what you can make of 'em?"

Giles's mouth fell open, then he grabbed eagerly for the pages, shooting a triumphant look at Wesley before heading off to his office to study them.

Buffy grinned at her. "This is your night for suave, Will. You should get captured more often."

"*No,* thank you," Willow said.

Wesley stood and straightened his tie. "Well, let's hope there's something useful in those pages," he said to Buffy. "The Mayor has the Box of Gavrok. As of now we're right back where we started." His eyes were unreadable. "Wouldn't you say?"

And all she and Willow could do was stare after the Watcher as he walked away.

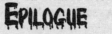

EPILOGUE

Willow found Buffy sitting under their favorite tree on the Quad, staring into space. "Deep thoughts?" she asked as she plopped onto the ground next to her.

Buffy smiled slightly. "Deep and meaningful."

"As in?" Willow waited.

Buffy picked at the grass. "As in I'm never getting out of here. I kept thinking if I stopped the Mayor . . . but I was kidding myself." She looked horribly resigned. "There's always going to be something. I'm a Sunnydale girl—no other choice."

"It must be tough," Willow said sympathetically. "I mean, here I am, I can do anything I want—I can go to any college in the country, and four or five in Europe . . . if I want."

Buffy looked a bit taken aback at Willow's words. "Please tell me you're going somewhere with this."

"Nope," Willow said. She pulled out her letter of acceptance and offered it to Buffy. "I'm not going anywhere."

Buffy gazed at the paper in her hand, not understanding. "U.C. Sunnydale?"

"I will be matriculating with the Class of 2003," Willow said proudly.

Buffy's mouth fell open. "Are you *serious?*"

"Say," Willow said nonchalantly, "isn't that where you're going?"

Her friend leaped at her and wrapped her in a bear hug so fierce that they both toppled over and onto the grass. "I can't believe it!" Suddenly, Buffy stopped and sat up. "Wait—what am I saying? You *can't.*"

"What do you mean, I can't?"

Buffy set her jaw stubbornly. "I won't let you."

Willow only looked at her calmly. "Of the two people here, which is the boss of me?"

"There are better schools," Buffy protested.

Willow smiled. "Sunnydale's not bad. And I can design my own curriculum."

"Okay," Buffy put in. "There are safer schools—there are safer *prisons.* I can't let you stay here because of me."

Willow folded her arms. "Actually, this isn't about you . . . although I'm fond, don't get me wrong, of you." She looked away, thinking. "The other night, being captured and all, facing off with Faith . . . things just kind of got clear. I mean, you've been fighting evil here for three years, and I've been helping out some, and now we're supposed to be deciding what we want to do with our lives. I realized that's what I want to do—fight evil. Help people." She looked back at Buffy. "I mean, I think it's worth doing, and I don't think you do it because you *have* to. It's a good fight, Buffy, and I want in."

For a long moment, Buffy said nothing, just sat there

looking quietly amazed. "I think I kind of love you," she finally said.

"Besides," Willow added, "I've got a shot at becoming a bad-ass Wicca. What better place to learn?"

Buffy considered this, then gave her a sly grin. "I feel the need for more sugar than the human body can handle."

Willow's eyes widened. "Mochas?"

"Yes, please!"

As they picked up their stuff and headed off, Buffy said thoughtfully, "It's weird. You look at something and you think you know exactly what you're seeing. And then you find out it's something else entirely."

Willow glanced at her. "Neat, huh?"

And Buffy smiled in return. "Sometimes it is."

Cordy held up the dress again, her favorite—black and sparkling, with a split up the left thigh, it would show off the best of her figure. *It would look so awesome, if only I could afford it, if only Daddy hadn't decided not to pay his taxes—*

"Chase, what are you doing?"

She looked around guiltily as the manager of the dress shop came out of the back and glared at her. "Your break's been over for ten minutes," the woman continued impatiently. "I still need you to restock the shelves and sweep out the storage room. Let's go!"

Cordelia nodded obediently and returned the dress to its place on the rack. Then she picked up one of the boxes on the floor and headed back to the stockroom to get to work.

There was no warmth in Angel's skin, but being held securely in the circle of his arms made her warm inside, and that's what counted.

Not the place couples usually went to be alone, but

Buffy curled up next to her boyfriend nonetheless, quite content.

Well . . . more or less.

"It's gonna be fun," Buffy told him. "Will and I are going to look at the campus on Saturday. I'm hoping Mom will let me live there—it's too far to go home every night, plus the lack of cool factor. Either way, I'll be closer to your place." She looked at Angel and smiled, got a tentative one in return. "I don't know what the stupid Mayor was talking about," she finally said. "How could he know anything about us?"

Angel stared into space. "Well, he's evil."

"Big-time," Buffy agreed. "He doesn't even know what a lasting relationship is."

"No."

"Probably the only lasting relationship he's ever had is with . . . evil."

"Yeah."

"Big, stupid evil guy," she said testily. "We'll be okay."

"We will," Angel echoed.

She snuggled closer to him, a little chilled despite his nearness.

And when Buffy glanced at his face, it didn't help that Angel's worried expression was a mirror of her own.

DAILY JOURNAL ENTRY:

Decisions are a funny and sometimes dangerous thing.

Often the smallest ones can change a life—like Faith, and her choosing to turn down the path to darkness. Or Buffy and Angel, choosing to stay together in the face of everything that seems so destined to split them up.

Or me, deciding to stay in Sunnydale for the long haul instead of bouncing off to start a new, and, as Buffy pointed out, probably safer college life somewhere else.

But somewhere else isn't Sunnydale, and while decisions are sometimes made in the space of a second, below the surface, if your brain's working right and keeping its priorities straight, there's a lot more that goes into them than appears on the top.

Yes, I might be safer somewhere else . . . okay, I would *definitely* be safer somewhere else. But there are things that need doing in Sunnydale, an ongoing struggle for good. And I want very much to be a part of that and to learn the Craft as best I can—I think I'll be good at it, and in the end, it'll be worth it. While I don't have the crystal ball part down yet, staying here doesn't at all mean I don't have any choices.

Yeah, I've got a feeling that there's a lot ahead for me, right here in the old hometown.

/PRESS ENTER TO SAVE FILE AND CLOSE PROGRAM/

ABOUT THE AUTHOR

ABOUT THE AUTHOR

Yvonne Navarro lives in a tiny town northwest of
Chicago and has been writing for hundreds of years.
Okay, maybe it just seems that way sometimes, although
rest assured that she's not in any danger of running out of
words. She has had eleven novels published, and then
came this one. In the *Buffy* arena, this is her second novelization, and she also authored the original novel *Paleo,*
plus wrote one of the stories in *How I Survived My Summer Vacation*, Vol. 1. She's written horror, science fiction,
mainstream, weird western, and even a little romance
now and then (though she usually has to toss a ghost in
there, just for giggles).

Her most recent novels are the suspenseful *That's Not
My Name* and *DeadTimes*. Her first published novel, *AfterAge,* was about vampires and the end of world (surprise!) and was a finalist for the Bram Stoker Award. In
her second novel, *deadrush,* she decided the concept of
zombies really needed revitalizing *(ow); deadrush* was
also nominated for the Bram Stoker Award. She's written
the novelizations of *Species* (for which actor Alfred
Molina picked up an Audie Award for an audiobook reading) and *Species II*, as well as *Aliens: Music of the
Spears*. She also authored *The First Name Reverse Dictionary,* a reference book for writers.

Currently she plans to write a sequel to almost every

solo novel she's ever written, and most of her older novels will see print again thanks to new technology. Especially under consideration is a sequel to *AfterAge*, as well as a third book to continue the unintentional miniseries of the award-winning *Final Impact* and its follow-up, *Red Shadows* . . . but because she has nothing to do in the meantime, she's working on a new horror novel called *Mirror Me*.

The intensely curious can find everything from book excerpts to artwork to pictures of Arizona, puppies, skydiving, and the Chicago academy where Yvonne trains in martial arts on her Web site, *Darke Palace*, at: http://www.para-net.com/~ynavarro.

Darke Palace also lets people know where Yvonne will be signing books and attending conventions, and where they can send books to be signed. There's even a message board—please visit!

Someday Yvonne plans to get another really big, friendly dog and name it something utterly diabolical.

"I'm the Idea Girl, the one who can always think of something to do."

VIOLET EYES

A spellbinding new novel of the future

by Nicole Luiken

Angel Eastland knows she's different. It's not just her violet eyes that set her apart. She's smarter than her classmates and more athletically gifted. Her only real competition is Michael Vallant, who also has violet eyes—eyes that tell her they're connected, in a way she can't figure out.

Michael understands Angel. He knows her dreams, her nightmares, and her most secret fears. Together they begin to realize that nothing around them is what it seems. Someone is watching them, night and day. They have just one desperate chance to escape, one chance to find their true destiny, but their enemies are powerful—and will do anything to stop them.

Available from

Published by Pocket Books   3074

"YOU'RE DEAD.
YOU DON'T BELONG HERE."

SUSANNAH JUST TRAVELED A GAZILLION MILES FROM NEW YORK TO CALIFORNIA IN ORDER TO LIVE WITH A BUNCH OF STUPID BOYS (HER NEW STEPBROTHERS). SHE HASN'T EVEN UNPACKED YET, SHE'S MADE HER MOTHER PRACTICALLY CRY ALREADY, AND NOW THERE'S A GHOST SITTING IN HER NEW BEDROOM. TRUE, JESSE'S A VERY ATTRACTIVE GUY GHOST, BUT THAT'S NOT THE POINT.

LIFE HASN'T BEEN EASY THESE PAST SIXTEEN YEARS. THAT'S BECAUSE SUSANNAH'S A MEDIATOR—A CONTACT PERSON FOR JUST ABOUT ANYBODY WHO CROAKS, LEAVING THINGS...WELL, UNTIDY. AT LEAST JESSE'S NOT DANGEROUS. UNLIKE HEATHER, THE ANGRY GIRL GHOST HANGING OUT AT SUSANNAH'S NEW HIGH SCHOOL....

READ *SHADOWLAND*

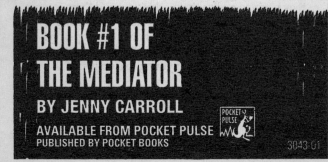

BOOK #1 OF
THE MEDIATOR
BY JENNY CARROLL
AVAILABLE FROM POCKET PULSE
PUBLISHED BY POCKET BOOKS

POCKET PULSE

3043-01